THRILLER NIGHT

WELCOME TO
PECULIAR,
PENNSYLVANIA!
A PERFECTLY NICE AND
NOT-AT-ALL CREEPY PLACE TO LIVE

WITCHES of PECULIAR

THRILLER NIGHT

LUNA GRAVES

ALADDIN
NEW YORK LONDON TORONTO SYDNEY NEW DELHI

This book is a work of fiction. Any references to historical events, real people, or real places are used fictitiously. Other names, characters, places, and events are products of the author's imagination, and any resemblance to actual events or places or persons, living or dead, is entirely coincidental.

ALADDIN
An imprint of Simon & Schuster Children's Publishing Division
1230 Avenue of the Americas, New York, New York 10020
First Aladdin paperback edition July 2022
Text copyright © 2022 by Simon & Schuster, Inc.
Illustrations copyright © 2022 by Laura Catrinella
Also available in an Aladdin hardcover edition.
All rights reserved, including the right of reproduction in whole or in part in any form.
ALADDIN and related logo are registered trademarks of Simon & Schuster, Inc.
For information about special discounts for bulk purchases,
please contact Simon & Schuster Special Sales at 1-866-506-1949
or business@simonandschuster.com.
The Simon & Schuster Speakers Bureau can bring authors to
your live event. For more information or to book an event contact
the Simon & Schuster Speakers Bureau at 1-866-248-3049 or visit our
website at www.simonspeakers.com.
Book designed by Heather Palisi
The text of this book was set in Really No. 2.
Manufactured in the United States of America 0622 OFF
2 4 6 8 10 9 7 5 3 1
Library of Congress Cataloging-in-Publication Data
Names: Graves, Luna, author.
Title: Thriller night / by Luna Graves.
Description: First Aladdin paperback edition. | New York : Aladdin, 2022. |
Series: Witches of Peculiar | Summary: The students of YIKESSS are invited to
a dance at the local public school, but they are prohibited from performing any
magic or supernatural acts around the humans.
Identifiers: LCCN 2021055803 (print) | LCCN 2021055804 (ebook) |
ISBN 9781665906258 (hc) | ISBN 9781665914277 (pbk) |
ISBN 9781665906265 (ebook)
Subjects: CYAC: Dance parties—Fiction. | Belonging (Social psychology)—
Fiction. | Twins—Fiction. | Sisters—Fiction. | Witches—Fiction. | Middle schools—
Fiction. | Schools—Fiction. | Supernatural—Fiction. | LCGFT: Novels. | Paranormal
fiction.
Classification: LCC PZ7.1.G7325 Th 2022 (print) | LCC PZ7.1.G7325 (ebook) |
DDC [Fic]—dc23
LC record available at https://lccn.loc.gov/2021055803
LC ebook record available at https://lccn.loc.gov/2021055804

THRILLER NIGHT

A widely believed myth among humans is that only witches and wizards practice alchemy, when in fact any supernatural creature with a proclivity for chemistry or botany can become a master of the craft. Take, for instance, Antony Maleficent. As a human, he was a respected pharmacologist who worked in a lab with medicines and chemicals. He also loved to cook, and as such, maintained a thriving herb and vegetable garden in his backyard. After the unfortunate lab explosion that turned him into a ghost, Ant took his skills with plants and chemicals and applied them to alchemy.

Ant traveled all around the world to learn everything he could, and then he settled in Peculiar, Pennsylvania, to start a family and open up his own apothecary—or pharmacy, according to the humans. He mixes, measures, and concocts all the potions and prescriptions himself while his partner, Ron, takes care of the finances. His twin daughters, the young witches Bella and Donna Maleficent, sometimes help out by unpacking inventory or stocking shelves.

It's a brisk fall afternoon on a Monday in Peculiar when one of the twins is doing just that.

Gray clouds hang low over the little black storefront at the end of Main Street, just past the Manor movie theater and across from

Bethesda's Broom Shoppe. A neon sign that reads ANT & RON'S hangs proudly over the door, enchanted with a blue light that will never burn out. Inside, the front room resembles a regular pharmacy, complete with aisles of human products, a cash register, and a counter where customers pick up their prescriptions. There's a small waiting area in the corner, where Bella currently sits on a lounge chair, listening to music and scrolling through her eyephone. She still hasn't changed out of her scream team uniform from practice after school.

In the back room, where monsters shop, Donna is unpacking new shipments of both the human and supernatural variety. She's wearing her own black lab coat, a mini version of her dad Ant's work uniform. So far she has catalogued antibiotic ointment, eye of newt, sunscreen, *and* Sunscream, and she still has four more boxes to go.

Dee tucks her curls behind her ear and looks up at her cat, Cornelius. He's stretched out on his back on a top shelf, batting a green dust bunny back and forth between his paws. "Can I get a little help here?" she asks him. "You could use your claws to cut the rest of the boxes open."

Cornelius looks at her upside down, blinks once, and then returns his full attention to the dust bunny.

Dee sighs. The whole reason she has extra shifts at the pharmacy this week is because Cornelius scratched up one of the paintings in the foyer, the one with the weird-looking elephants. It had been given to Ant as a gift by an old friend named Salvador, and apparently was sort of priceless.

Dee rips open a new box and removes the packing tissue to find it stuffed with snakeskins. She jumps back and wrinkles her nose. "Why couldn't it have been cough drops?" she mutters.

Dee hears a bell chime in the distance, meaning a customer has come into the store.

She moves to the door that connects the front and back rooms and looks through the small window there. She sees Bella on her phone, scrolling with her thumb and swaying her head to whatever music is coming through her earbuds, but Dee doesn't see anybody else.

"Dad," she calls out. "The bell rang. I think we have a customer."

When Ant doesn't reply, Dee leans back and peers through the doorway into his office. He has the phone perched between his chin and shoulder, and he's scribbling something down on a notepad. From this distance the makeup he applied to make his translucent skin appear less see-through almost makes him look human.

Dee turns to Cornelius. "I'm going to see if there's a customer who needs help. Be right back, okay?" She pauses by the door. "And *don't* break anything. If you do, I'm taking away your red ribbon for a week."

Cornelius gives her a startled look as she pushes open the door.

At first the store seems empty. Dee considers that maybe there's a ghost somewhere. They tend to make themselves completely invisible around humans to avoid any scrutiny. She stands still at the end of aisle two, listening, but hearing nothing except faint jazz music coming through the speakers on the ceiling. It's the "Smooth Jazz" playlist, Ant's favorite. If her pop, Ron, were managing the store today, they'd be listening to the Grateful Dead or Fleetwood Mac instead.

Dee is about to return to the back when she hears something coming from aisle four. She peeks around the corner and discovers a tall, gangly boy with dark brown skin flipping through a magazine. His curly hair pokes out from beneath his baseball cap, which features a logo of the Peculiar Porcupines, the mascot of the town's human public school.

Her eyes go wide as she realizes two things at once: the boy is the mayor's son, who almost caught her with Cornelius the night Bella zapped the cat back to life, and the magazine he's flipping through is *Haunted Housekeeping*, which was definitely not supposed to be in the front room, where humans could see it. She must have shelved it there by mistake.

Dee freezes behind the sunglasses display, unsure what to do next. Bella keeps insisting that nobody saw them that night, but what if Bella is wrong? What if the boy came here to tell them he knows exactly who they are and what they did?

She watches his expression as he flips through the magazine. He doesn't *look* scared or angry, or confused about the contents of the magazine. Actually, he looks interested. Then he laughs at something, and the sight of his smile makes every single bat in Dee's stomach take flight.

"What are you doing?"

Dee jumps and turns to find Bella standing

behind her with only one earbud in her ear. Faintly Dee can hear the chorus of the Michael Jackson song "Thriller."

"Shh!" Dee switches places with Bella and then motions for her to look around the corner. "It's the mayor's son."

When she sees him, Bella's eyes narrow suspiciously. "What is *he* doing here?" She grabs a heart-shaped pair of sunglasses from the display case and puts them on. A crease of concern forms between her eyebrows. "Do you think it has something to do with Cornelius? What if he recognizes us?"

Dee bites her lip. She's thinking about the camera on the mayor's porch. Could there have been others in the bushes that they didn't see? She picks up a pair of rainbow sunglasses and puts them on like Bella.

"Well," Bella says. "There's only one way to know for sure." She looks back at Dee. "We'll have to wipe his memory from that night."

Dee nearly exposes their position by laughing out loud, but Bella claps a hand over Dee's mouth just in time. "You can't be serious," Dee mumbles from behind Bella's hand. She pushes the hand away and lowers her voice to a whisper. "You know doing magic on a human without the approval of the Creepy Council is, like, *way* forbidden. And even if it weren't, that's an advanced spell. It's not like we can just flip open the handbook to find it."

"I'm sure we could find it in one of Dad's and Pop's old books," Bella says. Her voice is calm, but even through sunglasses, Dee can see how Bella's eyes spark with trouble. "Eugene could help us pick the lock on the cabinet."

Ant and Ron's second-floor study contains a number of odds and ends that are strictly off-limits to the twins, but nothing is more untouchable than the dark purple cabinet behind Ant's desk. Protected with three different magic-proof dead bolts, this cabinet is known to the twins as the Cabinet of Doom, because their dads have always told them that

9

if they ever dare to break the locks and venture inside, doom is what awaits them. Bella suspects the threat is just a scare tactic to keep them away from some really powerful spell books Ant collected while traveling the world to study alchemy, but Dee is slightly less certain. What if the cabinet contains an orb that conjures her worst fears, or a black hole that zaps her somewhere terrible? Either way, spiders would surely be involved.

Dee crosses her arms and sneaks another peek at the human. "He could get hurt."

"He won't," Bella says. "At least, not if we do the spell correctly."

"Have a heart, Bella," Dee says, shaking her head. "He just lost his cat! Don't you think he's been through enough?"

"Why do you care?" Bella takes off her sunglasses. She knows Dee has always been a softie when it comes to humans, but Dee has never taken such a keen interest in the well-being of one before. "He's just some random human."

"Excuse me?"

The twins turn their heads in unison. Standing in front of them is the mayor's son, holding the issue of *Haunted Housekeeping* and looking right at Dee.

CHAPTER 2

Do you work here?" the mayor's son asks. "I'm just some random human," he jokes, "looking for help."

Dee quickly removes the rainbow sunglasses. She searches his face for clues that he heard too much, but she doesn't see anything that suggests he's offended by their phrasing.

She gives her sister a discreet pinch that hopefully says, *Do not perform any magic on this boy in our dads' store!*

"Um, yeah, I do." She glances down at her black pharmacy coat. "I mean, sort of. Our dads own the place." She gestures to Bella, who purses her lips.

"I thought so." He smiles at Dee, the corners of his eyes crinkling behind glasses with black frames. "I mean, I've seen you here before."

"You have?" She feels the fluttering bats in her stomach again. "I mean, totally. You probably have."

"Did you need help with something?" Bella interjects.

"Oh yeah," Dee says, a little too eagerly, in Bella's opinion. "How can we help you?"

"Do you guys have the new *Howler* comic?" he asks. "I was looking over there, but I didn't see it with the rest of them. I did find this, though." He holds up the issue of *Haunted Housekeeping* he's been looking at. "There's some pretty weird stuff in here. Who knew there were over thirty-five different ways to hang cobwebs?"

"Everyone?" Bella mutters.

"Everyone except spiders," Dee jokes. "Their webs all look the same."

The boy laughs. "Maybe I should buy this for the spiders in my basement, then. They could definitely use some decorating tips."

Bella snatches the magazine out of the boy's hand. "It's not for sale." She looks pointedly at Dee. "There must have been a mix-up. *Someone* put this here in place of the new *Howler* comic, which means the new *Howler* comic is in the back, where this is supposed to be." She holds the magazine out to Dee, and Dee takes it from her.

"Right." Dee looks from Bella back to the boy. "I'll go check."

"Thanks," he says. "I'll wait by the register." He meets her eye and smiles, making her blush.

Dee hurries to the back with the issue of *Haunted Housekeeping*. A few moments later Bella follows behind, carrying the rest of the copies that had accidentally been put in the front room. Cornelius meows a greeting from his perch on the top shelf.

"Jeepers creepers, Dee. Count your lucky skulls that Dad didn't find these magazines in the front room." Bella drops the stack by Dee's feet. "He would've freaked."

Dee searches through their inventory of supernatural magazines until she finds the new *Howler* comic, shelved in the spot for *Haunted Housekeeping*, right where Bella guessed it would be. Dee pulls it out and examines it.

"These covers look exactly the same," Dee complains. She picks up a copy of *Haunted Housekeeping*, then shows them both to Bella. "It didn't seem like he cared, though," she thinks out loud, flipping through the comic. It's got spaceships with laser beams and aliens with purple skin. "It *seems* like he's into creepy stuff, just like us."

"So?" Bella furrows her brow, bored by the human reading materials and confused about her sister's interest. She looks at Dee curiously. "What was that out there, anyway? Why were you being so weird with him?"

Dee feels her face get hot. She quickly closes the comic. "I wasn't being *weird*," she says, avoiding Bella's intense gaze. "I was being nice."

"You were fraternizing with the enemy!" Bella shakes her head. If she didn't know any better, she'd think her sister has a crush on that boy. But that's just silly. Dee would never risk exposing the truth about their powers for a human . . . would she?

"Oh, give me a break," Dee says, moving toward the door. "If he knew about Cornelius, he would have said something by now. There's nothing to worry about."

Bella crosses her arms. "There's *always* something to worry about when humans are involved."

Comic in hand, Dee walks out of the room and away from her sister, slamming the door closed.

Cornelius jumps down from the top shelf and walks over to where Dee just exited. When he gets to the door, he meows and paws at it twice. Bella scoops him up, then puts his face to her nose and looks into his wide yellow eyes.

"She'll be back," Bella says, her words of assurance as much for herself as they are for Cornelius. "Don't you worry."

In the front room Dee hurries to the register, where the boy is already waiting. "You found it!" he says. "That's awesome."

She bites the inside of her cheek to keep from grinning like a big goof at having pleased him. "No big deal," she says, and puts the comic book on the counter. She tries typing in the code to unlock the register, but she fumbles over the keys twice.

Focus, she tells herself. Ron only just taught her how to use the register last week. She has never checked anyone out before, let alone a cute boy.

Moving very carefully, she types in the

correct code, then picks up the magazine and takes a deep breath before she scans it. When she presses enter, and the total pops up on the screen the way it's supposed to, she lets the breath out and smiles to herself. "That will be three ninety-nine," she tells him, feeling very sophisticated.

"Here you go." The boy gives her a five-dollar bill, and her heart skips a beat when his hand grazes hers. She's struck by its warmth—not hot like a werewolf, but balmy and just right. For a moment she forgets where she is and what she's supposed to be doing. It's only when she notices the digital numbers flashing *$3.99* and feels the five-dollar bill in her hand that she returns to earth.

Dee quickly enters the bill amount in the register, and the drawer pops open. "One dollar and one cent is your change," she recites in her best customer-service voice. She hands him the money the way she's practiced with her dads.

"Thanks." He picks up the comic, seemingly

oblivious to what just occurred. "I'm Sebastian, by the way."

"Dee," she says. "It's short for 'Donna,' but everybody calls me 'Dee.'"

"Dee," Sebastian repeats. "Cool name. Like Dee Dualla from *Battlestar Galactica*."

Dee blinks. "Battlestar . . . what?"

Sebastian grins. "*Battlestar Galactica*. It's a sci-fi comic. One of my favorites. It's all about the Colonial Fleet and their enemies, the Cylons." He glances at her from under the brim of his cap. "I, um, love books about space."

Dee smiles. "Creepy." She doesn't know much about space, and she isn't really a reader, either, but Sebastian doesn't need to know that yet.

"Creepy?" he repeats, a small smile forming.

Dee's eyes go wide. "I meant, like, cool."

"Creepy." Sebastian is still smiling. "I like that." He looks past her, toward the bulletin board on the back wall, and points to something hanging there. "By the way, are you going on Friday?"

She turns around to see a bright orange flyer with a pumpkin border advertising the Peculiar Public School's sixth-grade fall dance. "Oh," she says, blushing. "No. I actually go to YIKESSS."

Dee has never been to a real dance before but has always wanted to go. The human elementary school didn't have dances, and the closest thing YIKESSS kids get to a dance is the Creepy Carnival in the spring. The rides are fun, and the blueberry cotton cobwebs are *so* yummy, but there's no dance floor. Or humans.

"Whoa." Sebastian looks impressed. "A YIKESSS kid. Hey, I have to ask. Do you really have to take all your tests blindfolded?"

"What?" Dee says, trying her best to sound amused. "No."

As a matter of fact, according to the Spell Casting syllabus, blindfolds *are* going to be required during the Nocturnal Spells unit, but she decides to keep that bit of information to herself.

"Right," Sebastian says, laughing off his question. "Sorry. I'm sure you get questions like that all the time. There are a lot of rumors floating around about that place, you know."

Dee laughs nervously. She heard plenty of those rumors at the human elementary school. Fortunately, none of them came close to the truth. "People have really wild imaginations," she says, and then adds in a moment of bravery, "You can ask me anything you want to know."

"Really?" Sebastian smiles. "Well, maybe you can tell me more at the dance. YIKESSS kids are invited too. Didn't you see?" He gestures to the flyer again, and Dee takes a closer look. Printed at the bottom of the page, in small but bold type, is *YIKESSS STUDENTS WELCOME!*

Dee has hardly had time to process Sebastian's words when Bella appears out of nowhere with an eager look on her face. She was listening, Dee realizes, probably with the snooping spell she's been practicing.

"Jeepers creepers, we're really invited to the PPS sixth-grade dance?" she says, glancing from Sebastian to Dee. Like Dee, Bella has never been to a dance before, and her curiosity outweighs her general distrust of humans. Not to mention that she would never miss an opportunity to get all dressed up with her friends. "*Really* really?"

Dee takes the flyer off the bulletin board, her head spinning. Given that most PPS business doesn't apply to them, neither sister paid much attention to the flyer when it first went up. Now it seems that not only is Dee invited to a PPS dance but Sebastian *wants* her there too. Maybe he will even dance with her?

Dee's heart nearly skips a beat. She has to start practicing her human dance moves *immediately*.

Dee hands the flyer to Bella, who reads it quickly and then hugs the piece of paper to her chest. "I can't believe it!" Then she drops the flyer and looks at Dee. "But what are we going to *wear*?"

Sebastian laughs. "So maybe I'll see you there?"

Dee looks at the ground and smiles. "Maybe."

Sebastian leaves the store, and Bella and Dee exchange a look. After a beat of silence, they both scream.

Less than a second later, Ant is there, a look of terror on his face. He was so panicked by his daughters' screams that he didn't even bother to use the door, opting instead to float straight through the wall. "WHAT IS IT?"

"We're invited to a dance, Dad!" Bella tells him. "A human dance!"

Relief washes over Ant's face, and he puts his hand to where his beating heart used to be, recovering from the shock. "Girls."

"PPS is having their sixth-grade fall dance this Friday, and kids from YIKESSS are invited," Dee continues. "Can we please go, Dad?"

"*Please?*" Bella says.

"Girls, you *cannot* scream like that in the store. I thought something dreadful was happening!" Ant rubs at his temples like he has a headache.

"We're sorry," Bella says quickly.

"Really sorry," Dee echoes. "Can we please go?"

When Ant drops his hands, he has two translucent spots on the sides of his head where he smudged his makeup. "I don't know, girls. It seems like it could be dangerous. What if you can't control your magic and someone gets hurt?" Bella's and Dee's expressions morph into identical frowns, and Ant sighs. "All right, all right. You can go to the dance—"

Bella's and Dee's faces light up.

"—as long as Principal Koffin allows it."

Bella and Dee exchange a glance. *Would* Yvette Koffin, their strict harpy principal, allow her supernatural students to risk exposure by attending the human dance? It doesn't seem very likely. Add in the fact that Principal Koffin never told them about the event, and their chances seem even *less* likely.

The front door chimes again. Bella, Dee, and

Ant all look up to see a big purple troll duck through the entryway. "Afternoon', Antony," says the troll as he takes off his hat. "The wife sent me for some Dead Sea salt. Got any in stock?"

⌁⌁⌁⌁⌁⌁⌁ CHAPTER 3 ⌁⌁⌁⌁⌁⌁

The next morning the dark halls of YIKESSS are alight with chatter and excitement at the possibility of attending the PPS fall dance. Never before have the two schools mingled together for a function, and all anyone can talk about is whether or not Principal Koffin will agree to it.

On the bus Bella showed the dance flyer to Crypta Cauldronson, who promptly zapped it into a stack of flyers and began handing them out to the other students. By the time the bus got to school and the ravens squawked to signal the start of homeroom half an hour later, the entire school knew about the dance.

"I hope Principal Koffin lets us go," Charlie says in homeroom, their red eyes bright with excitement. They're sitting behind Bella, next to Dee, and diagonally across from Eugene at a desk carved from iron. All the desks in Professor Belinda's Spell Casting classroom were replaced with less flammable materials after Bella and Dee's accident on the first day of school. "I've been waiting for the chance to bust out my moonwalk."

"You can moonwalk?" Dee asks, looking up from the *Howler* comic on her desk. "That's impressive!"

"There's no way Koffin lets us go to the dance." Eugene leans back in his chair so it's balancing on two legs and takes a big bite of a breakfast burrito. "PPS has never invited YIKESSS to anything before. Why now?" he asks with a full mouth.

"Does there have to be a reason?" Charlie shrugs. "Maybe the human principal just thought it would be a nice thing to do."

Bella, who is attempting to study for an afternoon exam in Humans 101, snorts like that's a preposterous idea. In the front row Crypta Cauldronson looks up from her eyephone and turns around. "I heard PPS has a new principal this year. He just moved to town. He's a *widower*, poor guy."

Bella looks up from her flash cards and narrows her eyes at Crypta. "How do you know all that?"

Crypta smiles and flicks her shiny brown hair over her shoulder. "My mom. As president of the Creepy Council, it's kind of her job to know stuff like that."

"Oh, really?" Bella replies, trying to seem

nonchalant, though Dee notices that Bella is gripping her flash cards rather tightly. "If she knows so much, then why was *I* the one to tell you about the dance?"

Crypta scowls at Bella and turns back around.

"Nice one, Maleficent." Eugene holds up a hand to high-five Bella, still balancing in his chair. Suddenly a line of red sparks appears like a lasso and wraps itself around the chair's front legs. It yanks the chair back down onto all fours, making Eugene drop his burrito onto the floor.

"Are we going to make this a daily occurrence, Eugene?" Professor Belinda calls out from the front of the room. Her hand is in the air, and red sparks sizzle on her fingertips. "Perhaps I should send you to test out the chairs in Principal Koffin's tower, instead?"

Dressed in one of her signature floral maxi dresses and adorned with an armful of silver bangles, Professor Belinda looks like a harmless hippie. But to underestimate her would be a grave error, as she's the most powerful witch in all of Peculiar.

"No, ma'am, that won't be necessary." Eugene picks up his burrito and dusts it off. "Five-second rule," he says, and then takes another big bite. Bella, watching him, makes a disgusted face.

The raven in the corner squawks three times to signal the start of the morning announcements. It opens its mouth wide, but instead of another squawk, Principal Koffin's voice comes out.

"Good morning, students," she begins, and every ear in the room perks up. Is she going to talk about the dance?

"Before we begin with the day's usual announcements, I'd like to first address something that was brought to my attention this morning."

Bella and Dee exchange an excited glance.

"Professor Berry's fairymouse has gotten out

of its cage again," Principal Koffin says, and the entire classroom groans. "If anyone finds Twinkle, please return her to the fae wing immediately."

"That's the third time in a week," Charlie whispers, shaking their head. "They have got to get a better cage."

With a deep sigh that's audible through the raven, the principal continues. "By now I'm sure you've all seen the flyer that's been circulating through the school grounds advertising the Peculiar Public School fall dance, and the fact that YIKESSS students are, quote, 'welcome' to attend."

The classroom goes silent with anticipation.

"First, I feel I should share something with you all. I received this flyer in the mail last week, along with a note from the rather . . . *enthusiastic* new principal at the public school, encouraging us to attend. The truth is, I had no intention of addressing it. In my opinion, mingling with our human neighbors off school grounds is a situation ripe for disaster. With no magical veil to protect you, you'll be vulnerable. You'll be putting yourselves, the humans around you, and the supernatural community as a whole at risk. It's my job to keep you all safe. Why would I *ever* condone such an event?"

As Principal Koffin speaks, the students' anticipation deflates, and Bella's and Dee's looks of excitement turn into grimaces.

"But *then*, without my knowledge or approval, someone had the flyer distributed around town, at locations where they knew YIKESSS students would be able to see it. Now it seems my approval is no longer deemed necessary. The cat's out of the bag, as they say, and it can't be shoved back in no matter how hard you push, or how many spells you try—"

The principal pauses, presumably to compose herself.

"What I mean to say is that, if you want to go to this dance, I no longer feel I have the right to stop you. Therefore, you have my permission to attend, on the obvious condition that you remain on your best behavior. YIKESSS is not liable for any werewolf tantrums or magical misfires that may occur."

The classroom erupts into cheers.

"Listen carefully now." Principal Koffin sounds considerably less excited. "There shall be no magic or any other acts of the supernatural performed in the presence of the humans. *No* exceptions. Any student caught breaking this rule will be punished to the fullest extent. If you're thinking about ignoring this rule, remember: I will be there, and I will be watching you."

"You hear that, Bella?" Dee whispers. "No magic!"

"Yeah, yeah." Bella rolls her eyes. "I'll be perfectly boring."

"Tomorrow afternoon I will be hosting a school-wide assembly in the cafeteria that will be mandatory for all students who want to attend the dance. We'll be going over some rules for the evening, and it will be a chance for you to ask any questions you might have." She pauses, and then clears her throat. "In other news, auditions for the winter play, *A Midsummer's Nightmare*, will take place in the amphitheater after school today. Students wishing to . . ."

"Whoa," Eugene whispers over the announcements. "Seems like the human principal went over Principal K's head with this whole thing. Brave guy."

"She doesn't seem happy," Bella agrees, and then shrugs. "Oh well. I mean, she's still going to be supervising. How much damage could we actually do?"

Dee raises an eyebrow. Eugene and Charlie both struggle to keep straight faces.

"So we're going to meet at the witches' house before the dance, right?" Charlie says, switching gears.

"Of course." Bella puts away her flash cards, now having much more pressing matters to discuss. "And we all have to go thrift shopping to look for outfits!"

Dee thinks about Sebastian. He said he would see her at the dance, which means he's going to see her outfit, too. She *has* to look breathtaking. "Totally," Dee agrees, and then blushes into her lap.

Bella catches her. "Why are you making that face?"

Dee doesn't meet her sister's eye. "I don't know what you mean." She flips to the next page of the comic. Bella watches her for a long moment, taking in the red face, the *Howler* comic, and the lie.

"Oh, for the love of everything unholy," Bella says, exasperated. "You *do* have a crush on that human!"

Dee gasps. "Do not!"

"Do too!"

"What human?" Charlie asks, leaning in to better hear the gossip.

"The son of the human mayor, who almost caught us with Cornelius," Bella says, her voice sour. "He was snooping around the pharmacy yesterday."

"His name is Sebastian!" Dee says. "And he wasn't *snooping*. He was buying a comic."

"He's pretty cute, if I remember right," Charlie says. "Is he going to be at the dance?"

"Charlie!" Bella hisses. "Don't encourage her!"

"I agree with Maleficent on this one," Eugene says, gesturing to Bella as he munches the rest of his breakfast wrap. "Crushing on humans is dangerous business. Sooner or later some truths are going to slip out and hit the fan."

"That's not how that expression goes," Bella mutters.

"Can everybody please relax?" Dee closes the comic book. "I don't have a crush on him. I just think he's . . ." She smiles to herself, remembering. "Creepy."

"Maleficents," Professor Belinda says from her desk. She points to the raven, which is still broadcasting the morning announcements, and then the professor holds a finger up to her mouth. "Shh!"

Bella turns around with a sigh and picks up her flash cards again. Dee listens to the rest of the announcements with a smile on her face.

CHAPTER 4

There's a palpable energy in the air when Principal Koffin arrives in the cafeteria for the assembly the next afternoon. Having little experience with human events in general, most of the sixth grade has shown up, bright-eyed and eager to learn the ins and outs of a real human dance.

Bella and Dee, despite having spent the last five years at school with humans, are just as clueless as the other monsters in the room. Peculiar Elementary School never put on any dances, but even if they had, it's unlikely the twin witches would have been welcome. Bella and Dee's classmates, and more specifically their classmates' parents, often did everything they could to keep the twins—whom trouble *did* always seem to follow—away from social events.

The YIKESS students quiet down as Principal Koffin walks to the center of the cafeteria and steps onto the podium that was magically erected by Professor Belinda. A moment later Argus the four-eyed crow lands on her shoulder and calls the room to attention with a squawk. Bella, Dee, Charlie, and Eugene are seated at a table nearby.

"Good afternoon, students," the principal says, smoothing back her sleek blond bun. Her voice is amplified not by a microphone but by the podium's magic.

"What do you think she'll teach us first?" Bella whispers excitedly. "How to beat the humans in a dance-off? What to do if there's a ghoul in the hallway?" She smiles at the thought, knowing how ghouls like to haunt highly populated areas to mess with humans. "I've always wanted to meet one."

"We're supposed to blend in with the humans, not compete with them," Dee whispers back. "Now shh! I don't want to miss anything."

"Yeah, listen up, Dee." Crypta, seated across the table from the twins, leans forward. "You'd better learn how to blend in with the humans, because you're never going to fit in with us."

Dee's jaw drops in shock. What is *that* supposed to mean? Bella whips her head around and stares daggers at Crypta.

"At least we're not going to give ourselves away, little miss Creepy Council Junior. You couldn't pretend to be human if your life depended on it."

Crypta rolls her eyes and turns her attention back to the assembly. While most witches start to show signs of manifesting their powers around age nine or ten, Crypta manifested much earlier, at age four. As a result she never went to human elementary school and has spent less time around humans than any of the other witches at YIKESSS.

"Don't listen to her, Dee," Charlie whispers. "You're the creepiest witch I know."

"Yeah, she's just jealous." Bella nudges her sister. "And besides, wherever I fit, you fit."

Dee smiles weakly at her friends, touched even though they're trying too hard to make her feel better.

Sure, Dee thinks, she may not be as smart as Bella, or as good at flying, or as quick to learn spells . . . but she's still a Maleficent. A *witch*. Whether or not she gets along with humans doesn't change that.

So why do Crypta's words still scratch like a wolf at the door of Dee's brain?

"I'd like to start today's assembly by asking

for a volunteer," Principal Koffin says from the podium. She looks around the room, waiting for someone to raise their hand. "Ah, Gregory Tremble. Thank you."

Everyone looks across the cafeteria at Gregory, a ghost. "Um." He struggles to speak, becoming a little more transparent than usual. "I—I didn't volunteer."

"Not to worry, I'm sure you'll do just fine." The principal extends a long, slender hand and waves him forward. "Come along, quickly."

Gregory floats reluctantly into the center of the room.

"Excellent. Now, Gregory. Pretend I am a human child. I have just approached you and asked you to dance. How do you respond?"

A few giggles emerge from various places around the room. Gregory's bright white eyes dart around anxiously. If blood ran through his veins, he'd surely be blushing. After several long moments of silence, his nerves get the better of him and he disappears completely.

The room erupts into laughter, including Bella and Eugene. Charlie and Dee cringe with secondhand embarrassment.

Principal Koffin is unfazed, her face like stone. "Can anyone tell me what Gregory did wrong?"

Bella's hand shoots up into the air. She answers without waiting to be called on. "He floated instead of walking, and then he disappeared when he got nervous."

"Indeed." The principal nods. "Gregory followed his supernatural instincts. For him that means disappearing when the situation gets uncomfortable. For a vampire it might mean shape-shifting. A witch might cast a spell of protection or diversion. You all understand, I think, where I'm going with this." She looks at the spot where Gregory disappeared. "You may be seated now, Mr. Tremble."

Bella and Dee feel a whoosh of wind brush past them.

"Here at YIKESSS you are encouraged to

follow your supernatural instincts. But out there, in the presence of humans, you must actively fight against them. I understand if this seems confusing. One day you will all be able to control your instincts enough to use them to your advantage, but for most of you"—here Principal Koffin looks directly at Bella and Dee—"that day is still far off. Therefore, at the dance, discretion will be of the utmost importance."

Bella sticks her hand straight up in the air again. "What happens if we see a ghoul in the hallway? I'm *dying* for some haunting tips."

The principal gives Bella a disapproving look. "You will do nothing, because there will be no ghouls, gremlins, poltergeists, or the like haunting the halls that night."

Bella looks skeptical. "How do you know? The handbook says ghouls like to hang out in schools and hospitals."

Principal Koffin nods. "That's right. But fortunately for you students, Professor Belinda is already hard at work on a magical veil of protection that will keep such creatures at bay. It will be placed over PPS on Friday."

"Similar to our own protective veil, think of this one as a safety blanket." Professor Belinda speaks up. She's standing with Vice Principal Archaic and a few other members of the faculty by the door. "It will snuff out sparks of magic, put a glamour over supernatural traits like wings or extra eyes, and repel malevolent creatures."

"Uh-oh, Crypta," Bella says over her shoulder. "No malevolent creatures. That means you won't be able to get in."

Next to Bella, Eugene laughs.

Crypta sends red sparks shooting out of her finger and right into Bella's book bag, knocking it off the table and spilling its contents all over the floor. "Oops." Crypta shrugs. "My finger slipped."

"My Divination flash cards!" Bella frets, kneeling down while Dee glares at Crypta. "They were in alphabetical order."

From his perch on Principal Koffin's

shoulder, Argus flaps his wings toward Bella and Crypta and lets out a squawk to quiet them down. The principal turns her attention back to Professor Belinda.

"Let's continue. Professor, the music, please."

Professor Belinda sends blue sparks into the air, and a popular song by a human band starts playing from nowhere and everywhere.

"In order to act with discretion," Principal Koffin says over the music, "you must learn to partake in appropriate human dance. For many of you that will require a certain reining in of strength and skill. For instance, Wendy Fang—"

Everyone turns to look at Wendy, a werewolf who's on the scream team with Bella and Crypta and is known for her ability to land backflips from the top of the pyramid. She stands up timidly.

"Please show me how you might normally dance."

Wendy laughs and looks around uncomfortably. "By myself?"

"Certainly not," Principal Koffin says, and then lifts her wings off her back. "I'll dance with you."

The principal flies into the air and then starts swaying her hips to the beat, ignoring the waves of laughter coming from the students. Wendy, looking uncertain, forcefully starts bobbing her head.

"Come on, give it your all," Principal Koffin says, spinning around in the air.

Wendy starts dancing for real, throwing her whole body into the beat and jumping around. Eventually she jumps so high that she does two consecutive backflips. When she lands on her feet, the cafeteria bursts into cheers and applause, and Wendy lets out a long howl of satisfaction.

The music stops and Principal Koffin returns to the podium, composing herself. "Thank you, Wendy. That was a perfect example of what *not* to do at the dance."

Wendy's smile fades, and she quickly sits back down.

"You see," the principal continues, "human children can't jump that high, and they definitely can't do aerial tricks. You'll all have to restrain yourselves to the floor, I'm afraid."

Collective groans move across the cafeteria. In the back a pink hand is raised in the air. "What do human dance moves look like, exactly?" the hand's owner says.

"I'm glad you asked." Principal Koffin nods at Professor Belinda, and the music starts up again. "I will now demonstrate some acceptable human dance moves. First we have the sprinkler." She puts one hand behind her head and stretches the other one out in front, then moves her arm to the beat. "Next, the shopping cart." She puts both hands in front of her like she's holding a cart handle, then rhythmically extends her arms as if she's grabbing items off a shelf. "Another is the chicken dance."

Bella wrinkles her nose. "Her moves are a little outdated, don't you think?"

"I kind of like this one," Charlie says, shimmying their shoulders. Principal Koffin has moved on to the jazz square.

After a few more questionable dance moves, Professor Belinda changes the music to a slower song, and Principal Koffin splits the room into groups. "Find a partner," the principal instructs the students. "One of you place your hands on your partner's shoulders, and the other put your hands on your partner's waist, far away, like so." She holds her arms all the way out in front of her. "Some humans call it leaving room for the holy spirit, which is absurd, of course, as spirits do not enjoy dancing to loud music."

Everyone stands up. Eugene looks at Bella. "What do you say, Maleficent? Want to be partners?"

"Sorry." Bella links arms with Dee. "Dee and I are always partners."

Dee smiles apologetically at Charlie, who was clearly about to suggest partnering up. "Next time?"

Charlie shrugs like it's no big deal and then turns to Eugene. "Partners?"

Eugene plops his hands onto Charlie's shoulders. "Sorry if I step on your feet," he says. "I've never danced like this before. I *can* do a pretty wicked worm, though."

"The worm? That's cute," Charlie says. "Did I mention I could moonwalk—"

"*Yes,*" Eugene interrupts.

"—upside down? Only in bat form, but I'm still working on it."

Eugene's pointy ears droop just a little. "Show-off."

Bella's hands go onto Dee's shoulders, and Dee's hands to Bella's waist. They start swaying back and forth.

"What do you mean, 'next time'?" Bella asks, referring to what Dee said to Charlie. Dee can hear the hurt in her voice. "You and I pinky-swore we'd always be partners."

"I know," Dee says. "But don't you think it might be good for us to partner with other monsters sometimes? You know, to meet new friends?"

Bella makes a face. "What do I need new friends for? I have you."

"Ow!" Charlie yelps next to the twins. "My foot!"

"Sorry." Eugene shrugs. "At least I warned you."

Dee bites her lip, unable to meet her sister's eye. "I just think, if we want to fit in, we should get to know other people too."

Bella's eyes spark with recognition. "You're still thinking about what Crypta said." She shakes her sister's shoulders, urging her to snap out of it. "Dee, seriously, don't listen to her. You're a witch. Of course you fit in."

"But maybe she has a point," Dee falters. "I mean, it doesn't really *feel* like I fit in. Besides Charlie and Eugene, I don't know anybody else here. At least you've got friends on the scream team."

Dee thinks about Sebastian again, about the easy way they fell into conversation at the pharmacy. She has always had an easier time relating to humans than other monsters.

"The girls on the scream team aren't my friends," Bella insists. "They're, like, my colleagues. I just need them to like me so they'll vote me captain."

Suddenly the music stops playing. "Great work, everyone," Principal Koffin calls out from the podium. "Now return to your seats, and we'll discuss the human oddities otherwise known as corsages and boutonnieres."

Bella squeezes Dee's shoulders. "Don't worry, Dee. You've got plenty of time to find a place for yourself." Then the sisters break apart. "It's all going to work out. You'll see."

CHAPTER 5

After school on Friday, Bella and Dee rush back to their home in Eerie Estates to get ready for the dance. Thanks to their pop Ron's keen decorative eye, the girls' bedroom resembles a beautiful nightmare, perfectly suited for a couple of blossoming witches. Their beds are adorned with iron headboards and dark canopies that sparkle like the night sky. The deep purple walls and black shag rug are magic-absorbent, so any spells that might accidentally ricochet and make a mess will instead sink in and disappear. Plus, each sister has her own personalized casting vanity and cauldron, hot pink for Bella and green for Dee. The witchy possibilities are endless.

Their dads have already agreed to let Charlie and Eugene come over early on the condition that the twins clean their room first, so Bella conjures a dusting charm and gathers old cups of water while Dee picks up dirty clothes from the floor and puts them into the hamper. Cornelius, meanwhile, chases and swats at his red ribbon, which Dee has enchanted to move around on its own. Then the twins play a round of rock, spider, scissors to see who has to vacuum the floor.

"Spider covers rock," Bella says. "I win."

Dee groans. "Best two out of three?"

Bella grins and shakes her head.

When their room is clean, Bella blasts some music while Dee pulls their outfits out of the closet and drapes them across her bed. Cornelius promptly stops playing with his ribbon to jump onto Dee's dress and curl into a little ball.

Bella picks up her outfit, a sharp pair of overalls with black and green pinstripes, and a turtleneck underneath—"Beetlejuice chic," Dee declared the look when Bella stepped out of the dressing room at the thrift store. With her favorite black leather booties and her crescent moon necklace, Bella thought she looked *very* chic, indeed. She taps herself on the shoulder, conjuring purple sparks and zapping the outfit onto her body. The uniform she was wearing replaces the overalls on the bed.

"Eek!" Bella squeals, spinning around to look at herself in the mirror. "We are going to be the creepiest witches at the dance."

"You mean the coolest," Dee reminds her, fiddling with her own star necklace. "That's what the humans would say."

"So what?" Bella fixes the part in her straight black hair so it's centered. "You can spend your whole life worrying about what every human thinks of you, or you can choose not to care, like me."

Dee purses her lips. Part of her knows Bella is right, that she shouldn't care what every human thinks of her, but another part of her recognizes that for the first time in their lives, Bella doesn't quite understand what Dee is going through. Bella is the perfect witch: strong, smart, and brave. She doesn't have to worry about fitting in with the humans because she already fits in so well with the monsters. Unlike Dee, Bella is sure of her place in the world.

Not to mention the fact that Dee actually *likes* humans. She's pretty sure she wants to work in the human world as a meteorologist one day, now that her talent for controlling the weather and conjuring natural disasters has been revealed, but she hasn't told Bella yet.

56

Choosing a life away from witchcraft is some-thing her sister *definitely* wouldn't understand.

Dee scoops up Cornelius and puts him on her pillow, then brushes the cat hair off her dress and zaps it onto her body the same way Bella put on her outfit. It's got green and black stripes, just like Bella's overalls, plus sheer green sleeves that sparkle and a bright green tutu skirt. When she spins, the skirt billows out around her knees and the sparkles gleam in the light. Best of all, it even has pockets.

She approaches the mirror, looks at her reflection next to Bella, and takes a deep breath. She wonders if Sebastian will think her dress is as "cool" as she does.

"Wait," Bella says, studying Dee's reflection. She moves behind Dee and starts fussing with her sister's curls, taking two handfuls of hair from the sides of her head and braiding them together to create a fancy half-up, half-down style. Then she puts her hands over Dee's head and rubs her fingertips together, conjuring silver sparks that fall into Dee's hair like tiny pieces of glitter.

"There," Bella says, stepping back to survey her work. "Now you're ready to dance under a disco ball."

An over-the-moon Dee grins at her reflection in the mirror, then throws her arms around her sister and hugs her tight. "Thanks, Bells."

Downstairs the doorbell rings, and the sisters swap excited glances.

"Girls!" Ron calls out. "Charlie and Eugene are here!"

Bella and Dee run into the hallway and lean over the banister. Ron opens the front door, and their friends step inside. The first thing Bella and Dee notice is Eugene's hair. It's even bigger than usual, possibly the result of a teasing comb and his mother's hair spray, and it perfectly matches the orange sweater-vest he bought for tonight. He stands out against the black and blue tiles that line the foyer.

Beside him, Charlie's black hair is slicked

back with gel, and they've traded the dark dress cape they usually wear for a bright red one Dee found in the racks at the thrift store. "It brings out your eyes," she said, urging them to try it on. After a moment of hesitation— bright colors draw attention, and Charlie doesn't usually like wearing anything other than black—they agreed.

"Wow," Bella calls out. "You two look great!"

"You witches look pretty spooktacular too," Eugene replies, smoothing up his hair. As the member of the group with the most experience around humans, Eugene is the least nervous, and therefore not very worried about blending in.

"Hi there," says a voice. A moment later Bella and Dee spot a woman in high-waisted jeans and a T-shirt moving slowly through the doorway. The twins take a closer look and realize that half her jaw and a cheekbone are poking out of her skin.

"I'm Vicky, and this is my husband, Ted." Ted sticks his head through the doorway and waves a pale, skeletal hand. "We're Eugene's parents."

"They *insisted* on coming along to take pictures," Eugene says, rolling his eyes.

"As they should," Ron says. He shakes both their hands. "Nice to meet you. I'm Ron. My husband, Antony, should be here any minute."

"Hey, creepy Halloween decorations, Mr. M," Charlie says, looking around the foyer and into the living room. The holiday is still weeks away, but the Maleficents take Halloween very seriously and like to decorate early. Their home, which is usually adorned with dark and mystical artifacts, gets transformed into a monster's worst night terror around the holidays. Picture lots of pastels, rustic wooden signs, and plenty of cute figurines of creatures and humans hugging.

"Thanks, Charlie." Ron smiles, though it's kind of hard to tell behind his bushy werewolf facial hair. He points to a big wooden sign above the fireplace that says LIVE, LAUGH, LOVE in cursive. "The girls picked that one out."

"Super scary," Eugene agrees. He picks up a smaller sign on the table by the door that says HOME IS WHERE THE HEART IS. "This one too."

Bella and Dee join everyone downstairs, with Cornelius not far behind. "Dee!" Charlie gasps when they see her. "You're so sparkly!"

"It was Bella's idea." Dee spins in a circle, letting her dress and hair shimmer in the light.

Bella grins. "I used a sparkle charm."

"You two look so beautiful." Ron puts a hairy hand to his chest and shakes his head in disbelief. "I can't believe you're going to your first dance. Where did the time go?"

"Don't cry, Pop!" Dee hugs him around his waist. "If you cry, I'll cry!"

"I'm *not* crying," Ron says, and then turns his head to discreetly wipe a tear from his cheek.

"Oh, jeepers." Bella rolls her eyes. Dee is only five minutes younger, but sometimes Bella thinks it feels more like five years. "We're only going to be gone for two hours."

Eugene takes a step forward. "Hey, witches,

check this out." He pulls something out of his pocket, a little black box with a red button on top.

"What is it?" Bella asks. "Jewelry?"

"Better." Eugene smiles wide. "It's a 3-D printer. I programmed it to print a corsage that matches your outfit. I call it . . ." He thinks for a moment. "Well, I haven't actually come up with a name yet." He holds the box out to Bella. "Go ahead, push the button."

Bella raises an eyebrow, considering, then shakes her head. "No, thanks. Flowers don't really go with this outfit."

"I want to try!" Dee takes the box from Bella. She presses the button, then feels the box start to warm up. She hears some bleep-bloops and feels the turning gears. Finally the box dings.

"That means it's ready," Eugene explains. "Open it."

Dee lifts the lid and pulls out . . . well, she's not sure exactly. "What's this?" she asks, holding up some sort of purple-and-white vegetable attached to a ribbon.

"It looks like a turnip," Vicky says, leaning a little closer. "Oh dear."

"Hobgoblins." Eugene's ears droop. He snatches the box from Dee and starts turning it over in his hand. "It's supposed to print flowers, not vegetables!"

Ron shrugs. "Close enough. They both grow in the ground." He smiles at Eugene. "That's some really impressive magic, kid."

Eugene puts the box away, obviously disappointed. "It's not magic." He mopes. "It's code."

"It's still awesome," Dee says. She hands the turnip corsage to Ron and holds out her wrist. "Will you help me tie it on, Pop?"

Suddenly Antony appears next to Charlie, making the skittish vampire scream in surprise. Ant closed the pharmacy early so he could get home to see the twins off, and in his haste decided once again to float through the wall instead of using the door.

"I'm here!" Ant says, looking around at the kids. "I came as fast as I could!"

"You're just in time for pictures, hon," Ron says. "Meet Eugene's parents, Vicky and Ted. I'm going to go get the camera."

"I'm so pleased to meet you," Ant says. He looks at Charlie. "Where's your mom tonight?"

"She's still on a haunting in Mexico," Charlie says, noticeably glum. "Her assignment keeps getting extended."

Charlie is used to their mother traveling all around the world for work—as a banshee, it's her job to haunt the homes of people who are going to die soon—but this is the longest she has ever been away.

"We spoke to Esmeralda on the phone earlier and promised we would send her some photos," Vicky explains. "She's devastated that she can't be here."

"Will you take some pictures on my phone too?" Bella gives her eyephone to Ant, then backs up and fixes her hair.

When Ron returns with his camera, the group lines up in the foyer underneath the crystal-ball light fixture. Eugene throws one arm around Bella's shoulder and the other around Dee's, while Charlie, the shortest of the bunch, stands next to Dee with their shoulders back and their head held high to appear taller. Ron points the camera at the group and says, "Say 'skeleton key'!"

"Skeleton key!" they all echo with smiles on their faces as Ron, Ant, and Vicky start snapping photos.

Dee feels Cornelius pawing at her leg. He looks up at her with big, sad eyes and lets out a forlorn meow.

"What's up, buddy?" She bends down to scratch his head. "You want to come to the dance too?"

"Bad idea," Bella says, widening her eyes at Dee. "Or did you forget who's going to be there tonight?"

Dee feels herself blush. She *definitely* didn't forget. "Nobody will recognize Cornelius," she replies instead of answering. "I'll keep him with me the whole time."

"Take him," Ron says, putting down the camera. "Dad and I are going out for dinner, and I can't have him scratching up any more art while we're gone."

Cornelius meows in agreement.

Dee smiles and picks him up. "Okay, Corny boy, you're coming with me."

"You're just going to carry him?" Bella asks, eyebrow raised.

"If I had to guess," Charlie says, "I'd say the human school probably has a rule against bringing pets to dances."

"So we're sneaking him in?" Eugene's pointy ears perk up. "Wicked."

Dee shifts Cornelius in her arms and considers her options. She could bring a bag, but that would be obvious, and anyway, he'd get bored in there pretty quickly. If only he were a little bit smaller, she thinks, and she could just stick him into her dress pocket . . .

"I know!" Dee puts him on the ground, sticks her pointer finger into the air, and spins it in a counterclockwise circle, conjuring yellow sparks that sprinkle down over Cornelius and turn him into a tiny black kitten. Cornelius looks down at his fuzzy paws, then up at Dee. He lets out a squeaky little meow of approval.

Charlie gasps. "Cornelius! You're the cutest kitten I've ever seen!"

Dee picks up Cornelius and gently tucks him into her pocket. "There you go," she coos. She looks up at Bella and their friends. "Is everybody ready?"

"Yeah!" Bella claps.

"I guess so," Charlie says, uneasy. "I really hope I don't get nervous and accidentally turn into a bat."

"Don't worry, Charlie," Eugene says. "Blending in with the humans is gonna be a piece of cobweb cake."

One by one the monsters walk out the door, ready for whatever the night has in store.

~~~~~~ CHAPTER 6 ~~~~~~

When Bella, Dee, Charlie, and Eugene get dropped off at the dance, they're surprised to find themselves standing outside the Peculiar Public School cafeteria.

"The cafeteria?" Bella says, glancing back at her dads in the car. "This is where the dance is?"

"Where did you think it would be, Bella

Boo?" Ron asks through the window, and Bella's expression turns into a grimace. He knows how she feels about being called that in public. "The gymnasium?"

Bella shrugs. She hadn't thought about it, but she supposes the cafeteria makes sense, much to her dismay. It's not like humans can just conjure a ballroom the way YIKESSS does whenever they have events.

"I'm sure it will still be awesome." Dee loops her arm through Bella's. "We're going to be the creepiest witches at the dance, remember?"

Bella gives her a sly smile. "The *coolest*."

"The cafeteria, all right!" Eugene glances eagerly toward the entrance. "I bet there's going to be a *ton* of food here."

"I hope there's no garlic," Charlie says. "Otherwise, I'm going to be sneezing all night."

Ant and Ron blow kisses and drive away, and the friends begin to move up the sidewalk. They pass a small cluster of humans hanging around by the doors. Their outfits, Bella notices, are dreadfully boring, made of all the same light colors and flat, uninteresting shapes—the exact opposite of Bella's and Dee's outfits. Bella smiles to herself, satisfied. She and her friends are definitely going to be the best-dressed at the dance.

"Nice hair, soft serve," one of the boys calls out to Eugene, with a smirk on his face. His friends all laugh.

"Thanks!" Eugene says earnestly. He nudges Dee. "Did you hear that? That kid thinks my hair looks soft."

"No." Bella glares at the kid. "He's saying your hair looks like soft-serve ice cream. He's being *mean*."

"Bella . . . ," Dee warns, knowing where this is headed. "Don't make a scene."

Bella waits until the boy makes eye contact with her, then lets her hair fall in front of her face and does her best Bloody Mary glare. The boy, so smug a moment ago, jerks back, frightened.

"Jeez, Bella." Charlie looks a little unnerved too. "You've been practicing."

"Of course I have." Bella fixes her hair and returns to normal. "If I'm going to be the youngest Bloody Mary in history, I have to be the scariest, too."

They show their YIKESSS IDs to the human woman seated at the doors, and she lets them pass. In her pocket Dee scratches kitten Cornelius behind the ears to keep him calm and out of sight. It's not until they're all safely inside that she lets him stick his head out and look around. When he does, he squeaks out an unenthusiastic meow.

"Cornelius is right," Bella says, taking in the room and scrunching up her nose. "This is totally *blah*."

It's common knowledge in the supernatural community that YIKESSS events, no matter how big or small their purpose, are always something of a spectacle. Decorations are enchanted to move and change, long tables are filled with grand feasts on self-heating (or cooling) platters, and everyone comes dressed in their most sinister attire. This human dance is a bit less vibrant. The balloons and streamers sort of sag, and the snack table—which appears to hold little more than punch and pretzel bites—can't be more than a few feet long.

"Where's the disco ball?" Dee looks up at the ceiling. "I thought human dances had disco balls."

"Why did you think that?" Charlie asks, looking nervously toward the kitchen for any signs of garlic.

Dee shrugs. "I saw it in a movie once."

"Aw," Eugene groans. "The kitchen is closed! There's no pizza or ice cream here at all."

Bella smirks and holds up a finger. "We could always conjure some."

"No magic!" Dee whispers, pushing down Bella's hand. "Don't even try. Look who's here." She points toward the snack table, where Principal Koffin, by far the tallest one in the room, stands behind a large glass bowl, scooping some orange punch into a cup and talking to a man. She's wearing a black pantsuit, and her wings are tucked behind her back so that they look like a cape. Perched at the window behind her, Argus the crow blinks his two sets of eyes and surveys the room, seemingly acting as lookout.

"Who's that she's talking to?" Charlie squints into the distance. Like all vampires, Charlie has excellent night vision, but the man is hard to distinguish through the crowd, and only his back is visible to the group.

"Maybe the principal," Bella guesses. He's wearing a crisp, expensive-looking suit, and when he turns his head, she can make out a straight nose and a sharply cut jaw. Then Bella notices Professor Belinda at the opposite end of the table, looking fabulous in a chic velvet robe that matches her wavy black hair. When Professor Belinda catches Bella looking, she smiles.

"Note to self," Bella says, waving back innocently. "Avoid that corner of the room." The teachers would all certainly be watching the group's every move.

Eugene, more concerned with what's on the table than who is behind it, lets out a groan. "That doesn't look like witch's brew punch," he says, and pouts. He's right—witch's brew punch is dark and smoky, and it bubbles. This drink is just Sprite and pineapple juice with sad, melty globs of sherbet.

"Come on, you guys," Dee says, trying to keep the mood up. "We knew it was going to be a little different from what we're used to. That's part of the fun!"

"Fun for who?" Eugene mutters. "Not my stomach."

"I agree with Dee," Charlie says, adjusting their cape. "Let's try to have some fun. At least the music is funky, right?"

"Right!" Dee grabs Bella's hand. "Come on, let's dance."

Dee drags Bella to the center of the room, and Charlie and Eugene follow close behind.

As the friends move, they notice many of their classmates lingering at the edge of the crowd, seemingly too nervous to mingle with the humans. When the twins reach the dance floor, they realize that none of the humans are even dancing. The kids are just huddled together in small circles, talking loudly over the music. Many of them stop their conversations to glance at Bella and Dee as they pass. Bella doesn't seem to notice, but Dee does.

Bella spots Crypta in the crowd, wearing a simple black dress and flats. "Wow," Bella says, surprised. "Look who decided to dress like a human. I have to admit, I didn't think she had it in her." Bella meets Crypta's eyes and waves. Crypta ignores her, opting instead to whisper something into their classmate Jeanie's ear.

The song changes, and all four friends recognize it instantly. "I love this one!" Bella shouts. She starts dancing, trying out the sprinkler first, and then forgoing Principal Koffin's suggestions altogether and jumping around instead.

"Me too!" Charlie agrees, dancing in a jazz square. Dee falls into step with them for a few beats, laughing as she sashays in her dress. Then Charlie stops and shouts, "Everybody, look out!" They grab their cape, spin around, and bust out an awesome moonwalk.

"Oh yeah?" Eugene crosses his arms. "That's pretty good, but you haven't seen my moves yet. Hey, witches." He looks at Bella and Dee. "Check this out." Then he drops to the floor and starts doing the worm.

Bella laughs. Dancing with her friends *is* pretty fun. It makes her forget all about the boring decorations. She grabs Dee's hands, spins her around in a circle, and then dips her down so far that she almost touches the ground. Dee shrieks with a mixture of fear and delight.

When she stands up, they do it again, but this time Dee spins and dips Bella. A few songs pass this way, with all four friends laughing together and dancing without a care in the world. Dee is having such a blast, she almost forgets to look for Sebastian—though she can't help but sneak a peek every now and then, hoping to spot his curly hair or contagious grin.

It's during one of these "sneak peeks" that Dee notices a group of human girls glancing over and laughing at them. She looks back at her friends but can't figure out what they're doing wrong. Have they revealed themselves as supernatural somehow?

Dee stops moving and takes a look around. Everybody else is still standing in small circles, talking or drinking melty sherbet punch and acting like they're too cool for dancing. It's obvious now that Dee and her friends are the only ones dancing like nobody's watching, when in fact *a lot* of people are watching.

She feels a swell of humiliation rise up inside her chest. In all her research on cool human dance moves, never once did it say that the coolest move of all was *not* dancing. Then she takes in everybody's plain pants and simple dresses. She looks down at her own dress, which suddenly appears much too poufy and too green. It seems she got that wrong too.

Dee looks back at the gossiping human girls. One of them makes eye contact with her and giggles again, and Dee's heart sinks. She hears Crypta's words in her head again: *You're never going to fit in with us.*

Dee's face starts to burn bright red. She already doesn't fit in with the other monsters. Now it seems she's failing at blending in with the humans, too.

That's when Dee notices Sebastian. He's standing not too far from the human girls, holding a cup of punch and chatting with a friend. Dee feels her pulse quicken. When he sees her, is he going to laugh at her too?

Without a word to Bella or her friends, Dee runs off the dance floor and out of the cafeteria.

CHAPTER 7

In the bathroom Dee puts Cornelius in the sink and studies her reflection in the mirror. Her outfit, which looked so fun and funky at home, just looks childish to her now. Beetle-juice chic—what was she thinking? Humans only dress like Beetlejuice to go trick-or-treating, and even then they don't add sparkles and tutus. Of *course* those girls were going to laugh at her.

Afraid to get caught breaking the rules by using magic, Dee tries to shake some of the sparkles out of her hair. Then she yanks at the green taffeta lining of her tutu. None of it does any good. She still feels as silly as she looks.

She lets out a frustrated huff. How is she supposed to work in the human world as a meteorologist if she can't even blend in for a couple of hours at a school dance? Not for the first time, she's jealous of Bella's aspirations to be the next Bloody Mary. More specifically, she's jealous of her sister's certainty. Bella is meant for scaring, the same way a fish is meant for swimming or a ghoul for haunting. Dee's purpose in life is still much less certain.

She hears Crypta's voice again, seeming to echo throughout the room. *You're never going to fit in with us.*

With Cornelius occupying the sink in front of her, she moves over to the next one and splashes cold water onto her face. Then she looks at herself in the mirror again.

"Bella is going to be Bloody Mary," she says, her hands gripping either side of the sink. "What will I be?"

In the mirror a figure appears behind Dee. She's wearing a dirty, tattered nightgown, and her long, dark hair hangs menacingly over her face. Dee jumps and then glances behind her. There's nobody there.

"Donna Maleficent," the figure in the mirror croaks. "How may I assist you this evening?"

"Bloody Mary?" Dee asks, surprised. She leans closer to the mirror, so close that her nose almost touches it. "What are you doing here?"

Mary tilts her head to the left. "Whatever do you mean, child? You summoned me."

"Oh," Dee says, confused. She didn't mean to summon anyone. She only said Mary's name once, under her breath, when the lore clearly states you're supposed to say it ten times, with the lights off and a candle burning. She knows because she has seen Bella try it over and over. Could the lore be mistaken?

"Well?" Mary says, impatient. "Do you want my assistance or not?"

Dee looks at Cornelius. His eyes are wide as he stares into the mirror. He sees Mary too, but he doesn't seem afraid. Just alert.

Dee looks at Mary again. "Sure, I guess. But don't you have scaring to do?"

"Eh." Mary shrugs. "Slow night."

"Huh." Dee thinks about Bella. "My sister is *not* going to believe this. She's kind of your biggest fan." She glances toward the door. "Could I maybe go get her?"

Mary shakes her head. "Only one at a time. That's the way it works."

Dee frowns. *Now* Mary wants to follow the rules. "Okay, well, I don't need to scare anyone, but maybe you could give me some advice?"

Bloody Mary takes one step closer to Dee, so that her face hovers just inches from Dee's cheek. Dee sees her chapped, bloody lips form a small smile.

"Very well." Mary's voice is somewhere between a whisper and a growl. "Speak."

"Okay," Dee begins, inching away from Mary. "It's just that I'm at this dance with Bella and my friends, trying to have fun, but the humans are laughing at me."

Mary is unimpressed. "And?"

"And . . . well, I don't want them to laugh at me." Dee bites her lip, feeling something like shame.

"Would you like me to unleash my vengeance upon them?" Mary raises her hands and hooks her fingers so they look like claws. "I could take their tongues, and they will laugh no more."

"No," Dee says urgently. "No vengeance. I want them to like me."

"Dear girl," Mary coos, and Dee can feel her breath, hot and foul, hit her cheek. "Whatever for? You're a witch. Be proud of your power!

They should fear you, and you should revel in their fear, as I do."

Dee makes a face. "Yeah, but scaring is more my sister Bella's thing. I want to use my powers to help humans."

"*Help* humans?" Mary repeats, and then puckers her lips in displeasure. "How very strange."

Suddenly the door opens, making Dee jump again. Mary disappears.

Crypta Cauldronson walks in, carrying a little black clutch. When she sees Dee, she stops.

"What are you doing?" she asks, raising one perfectly arched eyebrow. "Hiding from the humans?"

Dee shrugs. "Something like that."

Crypta moves to stand at the sink next to Dee. She looks in the mirror and starts reapplying her cherry lip gloss. "Well, you're not exactly trying to blend in, are you?" She smacks her lips together and then applies another layer. "That dress practically glows in the dark."

Dee stays silent as she looks at Crypta in the mirror. Crypta, with her shiny straight hair and perfectly plain dress, looks exactly like a human. *Typical,* Dee thinks. Just as Crypta fits in with the monsters better than Dee does, she can blend in better with the humans, too.

Dee feels overwhelmingly like a failure. There were plenty of dresses that looked just like Crypta's at the thrift store. She even tried a few of them on. *Why* hadn't she bought the pale pink one with the bow on the back? That one was nice enough. If she had, maybe Sebastian would have spoken to her by now. Maybe she looked so ridiculous that he was avoiding her on purpose.

From his place in the sink, Cornelius meows disapprovingly. He seems to know what Dee is thinking.

"Aw, is this your familiar?" Crypta asks.

Dee nods. "Cornelius."

"My mom says most witches don't connect with a familiar until they're older." Crypta smiles down at Cornelius, making Dee consider that maybe she isn't as heartless as she seems. *Maybe.* "You're lucky."

Lucky. Dee doesn't feel lucky. She feels foolish and embarrassed.

Crypta puts her lip gloss back into her clutch and fluffs up her hair. Then she pulls out her eyephone and takes a few mirror selfies. The blue eye blinks with each picture she takes.

"What you said at the assembly," Dee says quietly. "You really hurt my feelings, you know."

Crypta furrows her brow. "What did I say?"

Dee stares for a moment in disbelief. Of course Crypta doesn't remember. She's never thought about the consequences of her own actions before, Dee thinks. Why start now?

Still, Dee presses on. "You said that I would never fit in."

Crypta snorts. "That's it? Lighten up, Dee. It's just a joke." She puts her eyephone away and checks herself out in the mirror one last time. "You're so sensitive. Are you sure you're a witch?"

Crypta leaves the bathroom. Dee stares after her for a moment, stricken. Then she looks at herself in the mirror, silently mulling over Crypta's question. *Well, are you?*

"*Meow*," Cornelius insists, judgment in his eyes.

"Don't look at me like that," Dee whispers. "If I'm not a real witch, then maybe I should just be a human."

Dee holds her own gaze in the mirror. She doesn't care anymore if she gets in trouble and has to leave YIKESSS. At least then she won't have to worry about fitting in where she clearly doesn't belong.

She taps herself on the shoulder and spells the pale pink dress from the thrift store—or one just like it, with pockets—onto her body, along with a pair of white ballet flats like the black ones Crypta wears.

Dee does a little spin, surprised the spell worked. The protective charm Professor Belinda put over the school is supposed to make doing magic impossible. Perhaps there's a loophole that allows her to cast in the bathroom, or in case of an emergency? Which, according to Dee, this most definitely is.

Dee looks at herself and sighs. She got what she wanted. She'll finally be able to blend in with the humans. So why doesn't she feel better?

Cornelius meows again. Instead of responding, Dee picks him up and gently places him back in her pocket.

CHAPTER 8

Dee returns to the cafeteria, but this time she doesn't join Bella, Charlie, and Eugene in the middle of the dance floor. She scans the room for the human girls who laughed at her before, and spots them by the punch table, refilling their cups. Without a second thought she walks over.

"Hi," she says, smoothing down her dress.

The girls turn to look at her, and then exchange surprised glances among themselves. For a moment Dee worries they might recognize her.

A girl with red hair and bangs is the first to speak up. "Um, hi. Do you go to YIKESSS?"

Dee hesitates. She looks over at Bella and her friends, who are all watching her with wary expressions on their faces. Then she looks back at the girl and shakes her head.

"I just started at PPS," Dee lies. "I'm Donna."

In her pocket Cornelius lets out a small, disgruntled meow.

"I'm Katie," the girl replies. She gestures to the other two. "This is Emily and Jessica."

Jessica picks up a cup of punch from the snack table and offers it to Dee. "I *love* your dress."

"Thanks!" Dee, pleased with herself, takes a sip of the punch and winces. *Blech.* It's all sugar, no fizz, but she smiles and pretends to like it anyway.

In the middle of the dance floor, Bella, Charlie, and Eugene have all stopped dancing. It's the most human they've looked all night.

"What is she *doing*?" Bella, confused and a little irritated, watches Dee talk to the humans. Here they are, having a great time dancing with the humans, *just like* Dee wanted, and then all of a sudden she runs off with no explanation. It doesn't make sense. "And where did she get that dress?" Bella's face falls. "We don't match anymore."

"It looks like the one she tried on at the store," Charlie decides, shuffling their feet. "The one you said made her look like a human."

"Because it *did*," Bella says. She sees her sister glance back at her and then quickly look away, as if Bella doesn't even exist. "It *does*." Bella crosses her arms, trying to disguise the hurt she feels.

"It's a downgrade, for sure," Eugene agrees. He's still slightly out of breath from doing the worm for twenty minutes straight, and his poufy hair has deflated and gone lopsided. Sort of like a melted ice cream cone, Bella thinks regretfully. "Hey," Eugene adds, "maybe she's playing some kind of game?"

"Like what?" Bella scoffs, keeping all ice cream thoughts to herself. "The Ignore Your Friends game? What's fun about that?"

"She's probably just trying to see if she can fit in with the humans," Charlie observes, shimmying to the beat now. "Dee wants to be friends with everyone. You know how she is."

I thought I did, Bella thinks. Deep down she knows Charlie is right, but at the same time, Dee being friends with everyone usually doesn't come at Bella's expense. Her sister never excludes her.

Bella lets out a huff of frustration. "I don't understand what's so great about being human. You have way less power."

"*And* way less responsibility," Charlie points out. "Not everybody wants to be the next Bloody Mary, you know."

Bella shrugs. "Not everyone can be. Charlie, you should know. Your mom is one of the best scarers in the world."

"Yeah, which is why she's still in Mexico and I never get to see her. Sometimes less responsibility is a good thing."

Charlie, fully dancing again, moonwalks right into a human. The person turns around, and the friends recognize him as the man Principal Koffin was talking to earlier.

"Whoa there," he laughs, and Bella's eyes are drawn to his teeth, which are bright white and perfectly straight, almost artificial-looking.

"I'm so sorry," Charlie says, taking a step back. "I guess I just got carried away by the rhythm."

"That's all right. Happens to the best of us." He looks around at the group. "You kids are from YIKESSS, right? Having a good time?"

The group nods. Bella takes in his PPS STAFF badge, hanging from a lanyard around his neck. She reads his name, typed in bold print:

PRINCIPAL OSWALD PLEASANT. *Aha.* They were right before: This is the PPS principal.

"Wonderful," says Principal Pleasant, seeming to genuinely mean it. "I think it's so important for our two schools to join together as one community, don't you? We have so much to learn from each other."

The group nods again. "Totally," Bella adds, cracking a small, private smile. If only he really knew.

"Well, I'm off to the punch table," the principal says. He gives the group a wave. "Until we meet again!"

The group stares after him. "He seems nice enough," Charlie says.

"Definitely enthusiastic," Eugene adds. "Like Koffin said." He looks at Bella. "Anyway, I think it's okay that Dee is doing her own thing. You know, it's sort of like how—"

"But she's *not* doing her own thing," Bella interrupts him, remembering where their conversation left off. She feels a new wave of anger swell up inside her. "She's doing what the humans want her to do. Otherwise . . ." She looks down at her striped overalls, which she picked out specifically because they matched Dee's dress, and she clenches her fists. Bella knows how much Dee loves that stripy green dress, and how excited she was to wear it out tonight. "Otherwise she wouldn't have changed outfits."

Bella feels her magic flicker on her palms, the way it tends to do when her temper flares up. She takes a few deep breaths and lets them out slowly, the way Professor Belinda taught her.

"What I was *going* to say," Eugene continues when Bella is calmer, "is that as a goblin, everyone expects me to become a trickster. But *I* want to be a pilot."

Bella and Charlie share a look of surprise. They assumed Eugene would become a trickster not because he's a goblin but because of how much he likes mischief in general.

"You do?" Charlie asks.

Eugene smiles proudly and nods. "I'm going to be the first goblin pilot ever. Pretty cool, huh?"

"Aren't goblins afraid of heights?" Bella asks. She's pretty sure she read as much in her Supernatural Cultures textbook.

Eugene sighs. "All I'm saying is that wanting to fit in with humans doesn't mean I don't care about my monster friends. It just means I have other interests too."

Bella looks at Dee again. She's laughing with the humans, sipping sherbet punch and pretending to be too cool for dancing. She appears to be having a great time without her monster friends.

"Fine," Bella says as the song changes. "If she's having fun without us, then we can have fun without her, too." She starts dancing just as wildly as before. After only a moment of hesitation, Charlie and Eugene follow her lead.

Over with the humans, Dee is laughing at a joke she doesn't understand. Emily just showed the group a short video on some app that seems to be a lot like WitchStitch, but without any of the magic. Dee wishes she could show them a video she saw yesterday of a ghost dog fetching an enchanted tennis ball in the sky. Instead, when they ask Dee for her username, she can only say she doesn't have one.

"Really?" Katie says. "Wow, you must live under a rock."

Dee shakes her head. "I live in Eerie Estates."

That makes the girls laugh, which makes Dee smile, even though, once again, she doesn't understand what was so funny.

Two boys join them, and Dee recognizes one of them as the human who made fun of Eugene's hair outside.

"Mike, Wyatt, this is our new friend Donna," Katie says to the boys. She turns to Dee. "She's *hilarious*. Donna, tell him the joke you told us earlier. The one about the witch garage."

"Oh." Dee raises her eyebrows. "Um, it was just that witches don't have garages. They only have broom closets."

The whole group bursts into laughter, and Dee takes a satisfied sip of her drink. She hadn't been telling a joke, simply stating a fact, but the humans don't need to know that.

"Oh, man." Mike nudges Katie and gestures to the dance floor. "The YIKESSS weirdos are at it again."

Dee turns around to see Bella, Charlie, and Eugene dancing up a storm in the center of the room. Everybody around them has taken a few steps back to watch—also, probably to avoid accidentally getting hit by Eugene's unpredictable worm movements. Dee even sees a few human cell phones out, recording the whole thing.

Emily puts a hand over her mouth, stifling laughter. "I'm not sure what's more embarrassing, his dancing or his orange Hershey's Kiss hair."

"Probably his dancing," Jessica says.

Katie shakes her head. "His hair, all the way."

The girls look at Dee, expecting her to weigh

in. Dee bites the inside of her cheek. She knows she should say something to defend Eugene, but if she does, it will just give away the fact that she's lying about going to PPS, and she can't have that.

"His hair, totally," Dee agrees. She looks down at her cup of punch, not wanting to meet their eyes. "It's, like, as bright and melty as this sherbet."

Everybody laughs, and Katie turns to Mike. "What did I tell you?" She puts a hand on Dee's shoulder. *"Hilarious."*

Dee forces out a laugh even though her heart is pounding. It didn't feel good to say those things about Eugene. It definitely didn't feel "hilarious." She puts her hand into her pocket, and Cornelius nuzzles his tiny kitten head into her palm, making her feel a little better.

"You're right," Mike says to Katie, but he's looking at Dee. "Donna, you should hang with us at school on Monday. We have an extra seat at our lunch table."

"What's your schedule?" Katie pipes in. "Maybe we'll have a class together."

"My schedule?" Dee hurries to think of something to say, but her heart is still racing, and her lies are catching up to her. "Um . . ."

She takes a step backward and feels her ankle collide with another student's shoe. She reaches out for something, or someone, to steady herself with, but nobody comes. With a shriek she falls backward into the snack table, knocking it to the ground and spilling the entire bowl of punch all over her pink dress. Cornelius, sensing alarm, manages to hop out of her pocket just in time to avoid the splash.

The music stops, and Dee looks up from her place on the floor to see that everyone, human and monster alike, is staring at her, their expressions varying between laughter, annoyance, and secondhand embarrassment. She doesn't look long enough to see if Sebastian is among them.

"Oh my gosh." Jessica rushes over and crouches down next to Dee. "Are you all right?"

Dee lets Jessica help her up. She looks down at her dress, which is sopping wet and ruined, and then looks back up and locks eyes with Bella, who hasn't moved from her place in the center of the dance floor.

The sisters hold each other's gaze for one, two, three seconds.

Then Bella looks away.

Dee runs out of the cafeteria and into the hallway, with kitten Cornelius right on her heels. Bella, Eugene, and Charlie watch them go.

"Do you think we should go after her?" Charlie asks, their red eyes wide with concern.

Bella shakes her head. "Let her new human friends be the ones to help."

The music resumes, and Bella, Charlie, and Eugene continue to dance.

CHAPTER 9

The hallway is empty, dark, and quiet, save for the dance music coming through the open doors. Dee rounds the corner to a vacant row of lockers and sits down on the floor. Cornelius catches up a few moments later.

Dee looks back down the hallway, waiting for Bella, Charlie, Eugene, or even one of the humans to appear and ask if she's all right. But they never do. She and Cornelius are all alone.

Dee puts her head in her hands. What is she supposed to do now? She abandoned Bella and her friends for those humans, made fun of Eugene, and then lied to the humans about going to school with them. Not to mention that she and her clumsy legs spilled the sherbet punch *and* ruined her pink dress. That's four strikes. If this were a flyball game, she would be out.

Cornelius meows and brushes up against the side of her leg. Dee scoops his tiny kitten body up in her hands and kisses the top of his head. "At least we have each other," she whispers. Cornelius meows in agreement.

Dee looks down at her dress and sighs. It really *is* ruined. And yet she's surprised to find that she doesn't care one bit. She much preferred the green-and-black dress in all its poufy, stripy glory. She should never have changed outfits to begin with.

In fact, Dee thinks, she should never have come to the dance at all. Of course she was going to embarrass herself—she almost always does something embarrassing! She was never actually going to fit in with the humans. *Why* didn't she listen to Ant when he tried to tell her that going to a human dance wasn't a good idea?

She squeezes her eyes shut and wishes she were at home right now. Or anywhere but here, for that matter. Preferably someplace that doesn't have fragile objects, as her clumsiness would probably cause her to break something there, too. Jeepers, she wishes she weren't so clumsy. She wishes she were something more graceful, like a princess, or a gazelle, or . . .

She opens her eyes and sees the turnip corsage on her wrist. A turnip! Turnips *can't* trip. They don't have legs.

That's it, Dee thinks, letting out an unenthusiastic sigh. She wishes she were a turnip.

And then—*POOF!* In a burst of green magic, Dee is no longer sitting by the lockers. It seems she is lying down, and perhaps maybe even rolling? She catches a glimpse of Cornelius, who has grown ten times his kitten size. He lets out a panicked meow, and it sounds low and loud.

Oh no.

Cornelius hasn't grown larger at all. It's Dee who has shrunk, and with a sinking feeling she realizes . . .

She has accidentally turned herself into a turnip.

CHAPTER 10

Cornelius approaches Dee. He blinks his big yellow eyes curiously and touches her turnip greens with his nose.

"Cornelius!" Dee shouts up at him in her squeaky turnip voice. "Go get Bella!"

Cornelius cocks his head like he's listening, but he doesn't move.

"Cornelius, go find help!"

But instead of finding help, Cornelius starts playing with Dee, batting her back and forth between his paws. Dee lets out a groan of frustration. Kitten Cornelius is an even worse listener than the fully grown version.

Dee tries to reverse the spell by silently wishing herself back to normal, but it doesn't work. Perhaps because she doesn't have hands to conjure sparks? Or maybe Professor Belinda's protective charm *does* work, but only on intentional magic? Dee sighs. Whatever the reason, it seems she's stuck.

She listens closely for any sounds of life approaching, but the halls stay still and silent. What to do now besides get pushed around and hope that someone finds her? Someone supernatural, that is. If a human stumbles upon her, she'll have to stay quiet and act like a turnip. Dee can't go exposing the supernatural community over something so silly—she's already caused more than enough trouble for one night.

Cornelius swats her a little too hard, and she rolls away from him, behind a trash can, where she gets wedged between the can and the wall.

"Cornelius!" she yells out, struggling to wiggle herself free. "I'm stuck back here!"

Grunting and writhing, Dee tries to move with all her might, but it's no use. She isn't going to be able to get free on her own. She pauses to catch her breath and looks around.

That's when she notices the spiderwebs. They're scattered all around her, looking shiny, taut, and sinister.

Dee's tiny turnip heart begins to pound. She thinks about the decorative spiderweb article in the newest issue of *Haunted Housekeeping*, which encourages readers to hang their webs in a disorganized fashion to create the illusion of decay. These webs are much too pristine to be decorative.

On the other side of the trash can, Dee thinks she sees four pairs of eyes blinking at her in the darkness. She squeezes her own eyes shut, trying to convince herself she imagined it.

It could be worse, she reassures herself. She could be down in Eugene's basement again, holding that spider doll. Or worse still: taking a Potions exam.

When she opens her eyes, something brown and fuzzy is standing over her. A dog? No—she's three inches tall. A dog would be much bigger. This only seems like a dog to Dee because she's so small. The fuzzy creature backs up, revealing eight long, hooked legs. It blinks all eight of its eyes again.

Never mind, Dee thinks. *This is the worst scenario of them all.*

She screams at the top of her lungs, and the huge spider rears back. Then a fluffy black paw comes from out of nowhere and bats her away from the spider, back into the center of the hall.

"Cornelius!" Dee cries, relieved. "You saved me! You're such a good boy!"

He meows happily, and then immediately resumes playing with her.

"Ouch," she shouts. "Watch the face!"

Eventually Cornelius rolls Dee to the cafeteria doorway, where she has the chance to observe the dance going on without her. Most of the humans still aren't dancing or enjoying the music, opting instead to stand around drinking icky punch or scrolling on their phones. It all seems so terribly boring to Dee now. She can't remember why she ever wanted to be part of it in the first place.

She quickly spots Bella, Charlie, and Eugene, as her friends are the only ones in the whole room who are really dancing, and Dee is struck immediately by how awesome they look. She sees other students around them, both humans *and* monsters, whispering and laughing at the group's over-the-top and outdated moves. More important, she sees how Bella and her friends don't pay them any attention. All they care about is having fun, and clearly they are. From where Dee stands (or rolls), they seem to be having a blast.

In that moment she no longer cares whether she fits in with the humans or the monsters. She fits in with her friends, and that's all she needs. Bella, Charlie, and Eugene are the creepiest—no, the *coolest*—ones at this party. They're the ones other people should want to be liked by. Dee could be out there having fun with them right now if she hadn't been so concerned with what the humans thought of her.

And who knows? If she had stayed true to herself, maybe there's a human here who would have liked her anyway.

Just then Dee spots Sebastian. He's bobbing his head to the music while his eyes scan the crowd as if he's looking for someone. Dee's pale turnip cheeks turn bright red.

It's official: she really messed up.

CHAPTER 11

When a slow song comes on and the humans begin to pair off, Bella finally takes a break from dancing.

"Why are you stopping?" Charlie asks, their cape billowing as they sway to the soft rhythm. "I like this one."

"Me too," Eugene says. He looks down at his

shoes and then glances up at Bella. Is she imagining things, or is he nervous? "Hey, Maleficent, want to dance with me?"

Bella's eyebrows shoot up in surprise. Hasn't she been dancing with him the whole night? She looks around at the humans, how they've coupled up to rock back and forth while holding on to each other, the way she practiced with Dee at the assembly. Then she glowers. Thinking of her sister makes her feel a fresh wave of hurt.

"No, thanks." She shakes her head, and Eugene deflates just a little. "I'm going to find the bathroom."

"Right," Eugene says, laughing uncomfortably. "Totally get it. When you gotta go, you gotta go."

"Keep an eye out for Dee," Charlie reminds her. "I haven't seen her in a while."

Bella resists the urge to roll her eyes. "I'm sure she's fine."

"A bowl of punch spilled on her," Charlie points out. "In front of the whole school."

"*Two* whole schools," Eugene adds, swaying in time with Charlie.

"She's a klutz," Bella says. "It's nothing new."

Charlie and Eugene look at each other, both clearly holding their tongues.

Bella sighs, exasperated. "Fine, I'll look for her. But I'll bet one of her boring human friends let her borrow another one of their *boring* human dresses, and they're off somewhere talking about . . ." Bella pauses, thinking. "I don't know, whatever boring stuff humans talk about."

"Taxes?" Eugene guesses.

"Maybe." Charlie doesn't sound convinced. "Or maybe she's hiding somewhere, embarrassed?"

Eugene nods in agreement.

Bella replies with a dismissive wave of her hand. Then a human girl with braces and a red bow in her hair taps Charlie on the shoulder.

"Hi," she says, her voice shy. "I like your cape. Would you want to dance?"

Charlie looks back at Bella and Eugene, who

give encouraging nods. When Charlie returns their attention to the girl, they smile so wide that both of their fangs poke out. The girl doesn't seem to notice.

Bella leaves her friends and moves through the crowd, not caring that some people's eyes linger on her as she passes. Following the signs for the bathroom, she wanders into the hall-way. She's about to turn left, toward the bath-room, when she spots Cornelius off to the right, by himself.

"Cornelius?"

The kitten doesn't notice her. He's too busy playing with something small. Confused, Bella gets closer. The object between his paws appears to be a vegetable, maybe an onion, or a radish? Then she hears a small, squeaky sound. It takes her a few seconds to realize that the sound is coming from the radish.

"Bella! It's me!"

Bella's eyes widen. She leans over and nudges Cornelius away from the radish—from

Dee?—and then picks her up and dusts her off.

"Thank *badness* you're here!" Dee squeaks. "Cornelius was making me really dizzy."

"Dee?" Bella says, squinting down at her sister. "Why are you a radish?"

"I'm not a radish," Dee says, more than a little irritated. "I'm a turnip."

Bella covers her mouth with her hand as she resists the urge to laugh. "Sorry. Why are you a turnip?"

Turnip Dee puffs out her cheeks. "I was embarrassed, so I wished I was a turnip, and then I became one, and I can't figure out how to change back!"

Now Bella does laugh. She can't believe she was worried Dee had abandoned her for the humans, when the truth was, she had become a turnip.

"*Ha, ha, ha,*" Dee mocks. "It's so funny. Would you *please* help change me back?"

"That depends," Bella says, smirking. "Have you learned your lesson?"

"Bella!"

"Okay, okay," Bella says. "But honestly I have no idea how to fix this. I'll take you to Professor Belinda." She puts Cornelius into the front pocket of her overalls and cups Dee between her palms.

"Thanks," Dee says. "And, Bella, I *am* sorry. I shouldn't have ditched you or changed outfits."

"Don't worry about it," Bella says, walking back to the cafeteria. "Although, you're right about the dress. Pink lace? That *bow*?"

"I know," Dee admits. "I think the punch was actually an improvement."

With that, both sisters laugh, and everything is back to the way it's supposed to be.

Well, aside from the fact that Dee is still a turnip.

Bella finds Professor Belinda monitoring the snack table, which has been restored to its former punch-and-pretzel glory.

"Professor," Bella says, and her voice wavers. Will Dee get into trouble for this? The rules were clear: they weren't supposed to use *any* magic on PPS grounds. And Bella and Dee were already on thin ice with the principal.

Professor Belinda, who has been dancing to the music with her eyes closed, spins around quickly, as if Bella has awoken her from a dream. "What is it, Bella? Another spill?"

"It's, um . . ." Bella glances down at Dee. "Well, I'll just say it. My sister accidentally turned herself into a turnip."

Professor Belinda looks surprised. "I'm sorry?"

Bella opens her palms to reveal Turnip Dee. "Hi, Professor!" Dee squeaks.

"Oh, my!" Professor Belinda's eyes widen. She takes Dee from Bella and examines the girl turnip between her fingers. "Hmm. Good overall size and coloring. I must say, Dee, it seems you're a perfect turnip! Well done."

"Um," Dee says. "Thanks?"

"So, we won't get into trouble?" Bella clarifies.

Professor Belinda shakes her head. "This is a

simple fix. Now, if you had turned yourself into a rotting turnip, *that* would have been cause for concern."

"Phew." Dee smiles, relieved. Professor Belinda winces.

"Gah!" She holds Dee a little farther away from her body. "A turnip with teeth! What an unsettling sight."

"Hey!" Dee squeaks.

Professor Belinda looks at Bella. "Come along. Let's move into the hallway, and I'll lift the veil of protection. She'll be a witch again in no time."

In the hallway a few minutes later, Professor Belinda recites an incantation that temporarily lifts the veil of protection, then changes Dee from a turnip back to a witch. Dee, once again wearing her green-and-black stripy dress, does a little spin, glad to be normal again. That is, with the exception of a new streak of green in the front of her hair, which resembles the exact color of the leafy green part of a turnip.

"Creepy!" Bella says, reaching out to touch the streak. She takes a step back and examines her sister fully. "You know, it actually suits you."

"A small side effect from your time as a vegetable," Professor Belinda says. "A simple turmeric-and-star-salt potion should turn it to black again."

Dee thinks about it for a moment and then shakes her head. "I think I'd like to keep it."

Professor Belinda smiles. "Of course. Very witchy, indeed." She turns to go, but then looks back at the twins. After a beat of hesitation, she says, "One last thing. As I'm sure you're aware, it is most unusual that Dee managed to break through the veil of protection, even accidentally. The charm I created was a powerful one. It should not have been possible to penetrate it."

Dee raises her eyebrows, while Bella looks down at the floor.

"I'm going to investigate how this could have happened," Professor Belinda continues.

"But in the meantime, I think it's best not to mention this little kerfuffle to Principal Koffin, hmm? She's got enough in her cauldron as it is."

The twins nod in unison.

Professor Belinda returns to the cafeteria, and Dee gives Bella a big hug. "I'm so glad you found me. I thought I was going to be stuck as a turnip forever."

"What was it like, being that small?" Bella replies.

Dee thinks about the spider behind the trash can and shudders. "You don't want to know."

Bella glances through the doorway into the cafeteria. "Before we go back in, I have a confession to make."

Dee frowns. "What?"

From her pocket Bella pulls out a small drawstring velvet pouch. She unties the drawstring, and the contents spill onto her palm, revealing a tablespoon or so of black salt.

Dee's jaw drops open in shock. "You didn't."

Bella's face is apologetic. "What if something bad happened, and we needed to use our powers to protect ourselves?"

Dee shakes her head in disbelief. Bella came to the dance with enchanted salt in her pocket, which shielded her from the effects of Professor Belinda's magical veil. "Wait," Dee says. "*Our* powers?" She checks the other pocket of her dress, the one Cornelius wasn't hiding in all night, and feels the grainy texture of salt brush against her fingertips.

Bella shrugs. "I didn't have time to make you a bag, so I just poured some in there when you weren't looking."

Dee knows she should be mad about Bella's recklessness, but mostly she's just relieved there's an explanation for what happened. The idea that her magic could be strong enough to penetrate the veil on its own would be frightening if it weren't so preposterous. She still has so much to learn.

"Should we go back inside?" Dee asks, changing the subject. The dance is almost over, but she's only just getting started.

"Yes!" Bella agrees, and then turns to go in.

"Wait." Dee glances around to make sure nobody is coming. Then she grabs a section of Bella's hair and tugs on it once, turning it hot pink. Bella gasps in delight.

"There." Dee grins. "Now we're matching again."

⤙⤙⤙⤙⤙ ☠ CHAPTER 12 ☠ ⤚⤚⤚⤚⤚

By the time the DJ announces his last song of the night—"Thriller" by Michael Jackson— Bella, Dee, Charlie, and Eugene are having so much fun dancing that they've all but forgotten about Dee's brief experience as a turnip. Even better, a few other humans and monsters have joined them on the dance floor, so the event is actually starting to resemble a real school dance.

When Eugene gets on the ground to do the worm, a circle forms around him, and everybody starts clapping to the beat. Soon Charlie moonwalks their way into the center, and after that a human kid jumps in and starts flossing. Before they know it, a full-on dance-off is taking place. Cornelius sits on top of a speaker nearby, watching it all from a safe distance.

Meanwhile, Bella and Dee spin and dip and flip each other, laughing the whole time. At one point Bella spots Crypta on the sidelines, watching them. Bella waves her over, but Crypta quickly looks away, pretending not to see her.

"Your loss!" Bella calls out.

When the song ends, everybody on the dance floor groans in unison. A few YIKESSS kids try to start a "One more song" chant, but a stern look from Principal Koffin quiets them down immediately. Then the lights turn on, and it's official: the party is over.

"Whew!" Eugene says, panting. His hair has gone back to its natural wild state, and sweat glistens across his green forehead. "I don't know about you ghouls, but I'm exhausted."

"Me too," Dee agrees. She looks around for Cornelius, who jumps from his perch on top of the speaker over to her shoulder. She tucks him safely back into her pocket.

"That was *amazing*!" Charlie bounces on the balls of their feet, still full of energy. "I feel like I could dance all night."

"That's because you're technically nocturnal," Bella points out, a little out of breath herself.

"So are you," Charlie reminds her. They look at Eugene. "By the way, can I still sleep over at your house tonight?"

"Yeah!" Eugene nods eagerly. "I've gotta get your opinion on my newest experiment. Picture this—" He holds up his hands. "A machine that reads books for you."

Bella puts a hand on her hip. "An audiobook?"

Eugene points at her. "No. This reads the book *for* you, and then you press a button and the words get transferred into your brain!" He looks around at his friends eagerly.

"That actually works?" Dee asks, intrigued by any invention that would make her homework easier.

"Well, not *yet*." Eugene grimaces. "But once I work out the kinks, it will."

Suddenly and silently, Principal Koffin appears behind him, making Dee and Charlie jump in surprise.

"It is time to clear the premises," she tells them. "Did you all have an enjoyable evening?"

"The best!" Dee says. She links arms with Charlie and Bella, who then links arms with Eugene. "I'm so glad we all got to be here together."

"Without using any magic *at all*," Bella adds with her most innocent smile.

Principal Koffin replies with a simple "Mhm." And yet something about the way she says it makes Bella and Dee suspect she knows about everything that went on tonight.

"Well," Principal Koffin finishes. "I hope you all have a pleasant weekend." She nods her farewell and leaves just as quickly as she came. For a moment they all stare after her.

"What do you think she does on the weekends?" Bella asks.

"Who knows?" Eugene says. "Frankly, I'm surprised she even exists outside of YIKESSS. The harpy is practically part of the architecture."

"I'll bet she's got lots of stories to tell," Charlie says, and the rest of the group nods in agreement.

With linked arms all four friends head for the exit. They're almost to the doors when Dee notices Sebastian standing nearby with some friends. Before she has time to think about what to do next, his eyes meet hers.

"Dee!" He waves, and then walks over. "Hey. I was hoping to see you tonight."

Dee feels the bats in her stomach, pumping their wings as fast as they can.

"You look awesome," he says. "I like your hair. Very *creepy*," he adds with a wink.

Dee blushes. "Thanks." Cornelius pokes his head out from her pocket and meows, and Sebastian's face lights up.

"Wow, what a cute kitten! What's its name?"

"Cor—" Dee starts, and Bella widens her eyes in warning. "Cory. His name is Cory."

"Hi, Cory." Sebastian smiles and scratches him on the head. Cornelius purrs contentedly, like Sebastian is an old friend.

Which is exactly what he is, Dee quickly realizes. In fact, maybe *that's* why Cornelius has been so grumpy lately. He misses his pal Sebastian.

"So." Sebastian glances back at his friends, who are clearly waiting for him. "See you around?"

"Yeah." Dee smiles wide. "You most definitely will."

Dee, Cornelius, and her friends leave the cafeteria. It isn't until they're outside under the stars, a safe distance away from the humans, that Charlie asks in a hushed voice, "Was that the mayor's son?"

"Sebastian," Bella tells them. "And in case it wasn't obvious, Dee thinks he's the banshee's knees."

"It's obvious." Eugene nudges Dee playfully. He looks toward the parking lot and points at a black car that resembles a hearse. "Hey, there's my mom. Let's go, Charlie."

Charlie hugs Bella and Dee at the same time. "See you Monday!"

Bella and Dee watch their friends go, and then sit down on a bench while they wait for their dads.

"What a night," Dee says. She pulls Cornelius out of her pocket and holds him in front of her face. "Did you have fun, buddy?"

Cornelius meows happily. It seems his interaction with Sebastian has brightened his spirits.

"That makes two of us," she whispers.

"I danced more tonight than I ever have in my entire life!" Bella swoons, and then makes a displeased face. "Although, I was really hoping to meet a ghost. I wanted some haunting tips."

"Oh, by the way," Dee says, "I saw Bloody Mary."

Bella's jaw drops. "WHAT?" She puts her hands on Dee's shoulders. "Where? *How?*"

"In the bathroom," Dee says. "I said her name and she just appeared."

"Jeepers creepers! I've tried to summon her hundreds of times, and nothing happened, and you get to meet her on your first try?" Bella's jealousy morphs into admiration. "You know, she doesn't come for just anybody when they call. You must have caught her attention somehow."

Dee shrugs. She didn't think much of it before, but now that Bella mentions it, Dee can't help but wonder: Why *did* Bloody Mary choose her?

Dee grabs two fistfuls of her tutu. "Maybe it was my dress," she says jokingly.

Bella laughs. "Probably."

A familiar three-beat honk catches their attention, and the sisters look up to see their dads' white car idling in the parking lot.

"You have to tell me everything," Bella says, standing up. "What was she like?"

"I'll tell you all about it in the car." Dee stands up too. "But first let's ask if we can stop at Scary Good Shakes on the way home. I need to get the taste of turnip out of my mouth."

Bella giggles. "Deal."

A man walks into a windowless room. He shuts the door and locks it before turning on the light.

A fluorescent bulb illuminates the bare white walls. The room appears to be an office, albeit a very plain one. The only furniture inside is a desk, three chairs, and an empty bookshelf. There is also a narrow wooden door on the back wall, which presumably leads to a coat closet. Since the room has no windows, it's impossible to know for sure what time of day it is. But judging by the dark circles under the man's eyes, and perhaps also by the way he has haphazardly loosened his tie, it is likely very late, or even very early. Either way, it has been a while since he last slept.

The man walks to the desk in the center of the room. There is a computer on the desk, plus a stapler, two framed photographs of a woman and two small children, and a brass nameplate. He removes the ID badge from around his neck and drops it just behind the nameplate. Both say the same thing: PRINCIPAL OSWALD PLEASANT.

He pulls a set of keys out of his pocket and unlocks the second drawer on the desk's left side. He rifles through the contents of the drawer until he pulls out another, smaller set of keys. Then he stands up and moves to the closet. When he unlocks the door, he smiles.

The closet contains only one thing: a large wooden filing cabinet—an antique, by the look of it. Each drawer seems to have its own unique set of locks. The man examines the second key chain until he finds the two keys he needs. He inserts the keys into the locks, turns them simultaneously to the left until he hears a click, and then slides the drawer open slowly. When he lays eyes on what's inside, he lets out a small sigh of satisfaction.

The device he removes from the cabinet is small, black, and rectangular. He pushes a button and a screen lights up. He pushes another button, and the device starts to ring. It rings and rings until finally a woman's voice, distant and muffled, comes through the line.

"Beta." The man's voice is hardly above a whisper. "It's me."

The woman speaks softly too. It's impossible to make out her reply.

"I know," the man says. "It took longer than I anticipated, but the wait is over. I found her."

The man is quiet then. There's a noise in the distance, a sort of rumbling that could be coming from a machine. He doesn't seem to hear it, or else he's not bothered by it. He is focusing very hard on what the woman has to say. Finally he smiles, emphasizing his sharp jaw and large, straight teeth.

"That's right," he says. "The banshee is in Mexico."

He starts fiddling with a ring on his finger, a large silver thing with some sort of crest engraved on top. He raises his hand to his lips and kisses the ring once.

"You know what to do," he says to the woman. "I'll see you soon."

WITCHES of PECULIAR

MONSTROUS MATCHMAKERS

LUNA GRAVES

A black cat in a green collar moves through the shadows down Franken Lane, his fur illuminated by the dim light of the crescent moon. There are no lamps on this street, nor anywhere else inside the gates of Eerie Estates. The supernatural creatures who call this neighborhood home much prefer the darkness.

At the end of the road, the cat makes a right onto Stein Street, then ducks behind a row of shrubs and disappears. It's his piercing yellow eyes that give him away again a few minutes later, when he emerges two blocks westward, on the front lawn of the black house at 333 Quivering Court. He walks up the path to the porch and then hops on the sill of an open window, where he can hear muffled voices and see the flickering blue glow of the living room TV. After pausing a moment to lick his paw, he slinks inside, and the window closes behind him.

On the other side of the wall, the young witch Bella Maleficent sits cross-legged on the couch in her bright green pajamas with a bowl of popcorn in her lap. She leans forward, her eyes glued to the TV. To her left, her sister Dee Maleficent slouches between two cushions, scrolling through her green eyephone while her feet rest on the black coffee table in front of her. The cat jumps down from the windowsill onto the back of the couch, and then crawls over Dee's shoulder to rest in her lap.

"There you are, Corny boy." Dee scratches behind Cornelius's ears and kisses him on top of the head. "I thought Eugene might've kidnapped you."

In the months since Cornelius has come to live with them, he's gotten quite comfortable venturing around their gated community on his own. Eugene even texted the twins an hour ago that the cat had shown up on his doorstep to say hello.

Bella reaches down absently and grabs a handful of popcorn, then shoves the whole thing into her mouth. *"Ugh,"* she groans between chews. On the screen, a woman with hair as red as the crushed velvet couch she sits on is pleading her case. "Serafina'll say anything to get a broom."

Dee puts down her eyephone and focuses on the TV. The twins are watching *Which Witch Is the One?*, their favorite supernatural matchmaking show. On this episode, Alistair must take two contestants on a single date and then eliminate the one he likes the least.

"I could really see myself falling in love with him," says Serafina, one of the witches chosen for the date. She's speaking to the camera in a confessional-style setting. *"From day one, I've trusted in this process, and I've been one hundred percent genuine. I think Alistair can feel that I'm here for the right reasons."*

From his place drying dishes in the kitchen, they hear their dad Ron snort. "Yeah, right. She's there to become WitchStitch famous."

"Totally, Pop," Bella agrees. She reaches for more popcorn, but her hand hits the bottom of the bowl. She uses her pointer finger to zap it full of a fresh batch, pleased when every kernel is perfectly popped, no burnt pieces to be seen. Since their disastrous first day at YIKESSS, with practice, the twins have been able to master simple spells with a much lower rate of chaos or destruction.

"So what?" Dee says. "That doesn't mean she isn't there to find love, too."

"That's right, honey," says their dad Antony, appearing in the doorway between the kitchen and living room. "We shouldn't judge other creatures before we get to know them."

"Come on, Dad, she *wants* us to judge her," Bella argues. "Why else would she have gone on supernatural television to find love?"

The camera switches to the other contestant, Helena. *"When I started this journey, my cauldron was empty. Then Alistair filled it up. I know it's taken me a little longer than most of the other witches here to let down my walls, but now that I have . . ."* She pauses to wipe a tear from her cheek and compose herself. *"I don't want to go home tonight. Alistair has my heart."*

"Why does everyone have to be so cheesy?" Dee says, checking her phone and then immediately putting it down again. "Nobody talks like this in real life."

"Love makes people do strange things," Ron

says, joining Ant in the doorway. "Look at your dad and me. I moved to the *suburbs* for him."

Ant smiles and shakes his head. "The Enchanted Forest was no place to raise a family."

"You were right," Ron says, putting an arm around his husband. Over time, ghosts naturally become more solid around people they love. In the comfort of his own home, Ant is so solid he can almost pass for human. "What else is new?" They exchange a quick kiss, and Bella and Dee both groan.

"Right in front of us?" Bella says. "Unbelievable."

"So embarrassing!" Dee adds.

Their dads look at each other and laugh, and the twins exchange a small smile. Bella and Dee would never admit it to Ant and Ron, but they know how lucky they are to have two parents so in love.

"Bed in ten minutes," Ant says. He moves across the living room, toward the stairwell in the foyer.

Ron shuts off the lights in the kitchen. "Good night, girls," he says, following Ant. "We love you."

"Love you," they both say at the same time.

Bella waits until their dads get all the way up the stairs before she smirks at Dee. She knows what her sister is looking for every time she checks her phone. Or rather, *who*.

"I'll bet you'll be just as *in lurv* as Dad and Pop after your movie date tomorrow."

Dee feels her cheeks heat up. Over the weekend, Sebastian visited the pharmacy while Dee was stocking shelves and told her about the new *Space Wars* movie that just came out. He said he was seeing it with a couple of friends on Tuesday afternoon at the Manor Theater and asked if she would like to come along. In a bout of nerves, Dee stammered that *actually*, she and her friends were planning to see that movie on Tuesday too. What were the odds! They agreed to meet there and then exchanged phone numbers, *just in case*. So far, she hasn't received so much as a text, but that could change at any moment.

"It's not a *date*," Dee says, stroking Cornelius's back and smiling to herself. "It's a friendly gathering. That's why you're coming."

"Right," Bella says. "And I'll be there for you, of course. But Dee, you know you don't need me. You never have trouble thinking of what to say when Sebastian comes to visit you at the pharmacy."

"I know," Dee says. "But that's when it's just the two of us. This time, his human friends will be there. What if I say the wrong thing?"

"You won't," Bella assures her. "Charlie and Eugene, on the other hand—"

Hearing Eugene's name, Cornelius lifts his head and meows. He gives Dee a meaningful look.

"What is it, buddy?" Dee looks at Bella. "I think he needs to tell us something about Eugene."

"Wait, Alistair is about to give out his broom!" Bella squeals, returning her full attention to the TV, where the three witches are seated on a picnic blanket in the woods. "He can tell us during the commercial."

"This was not an easy decision to make," says Alistair in an accent veering toward Hungarian. *"You've both sacrificed so much to come on this journey with me, and you've trusted the process even through times of uncertainty. Serafina, I love how easily we click. You make me laugh, and we have so much fun together, but there's still a part of me that worries you're not ready for commitment. And Helena, it has been such an incredible experience getting to know you. I've seen how much you've tried to open up these last couple of weeks, and I've appreciated—"*

"Jeepers creepers," Bella groans. "Get on with it already!"

"But I do feel like there's still a part of you that you're holding back. You've lowered your walls, but you haven't knocked them down completely. I need a witch who isn't afraid to show me who they really are. That being said . . ." Alistair turns to Serafina. *"Serafina, will you accept this broom?"*

Bella and Dee gasp. A kernel of popcorn falls out of Bella's mouth.

Serafina smiles wide. *"I will."* She takes the red broom. Then Alistair picks up his own broom and the two fly away together holding hands, leaving Helena behind as she bursts into tears. The show cuts to commercial.

"No, he didn't!" Bella says, at the same time Dee says, "Big mistake, Alistair!"

"Meow!" Cornelius insists, looking from Dee to Bella.

"Okay, okay." Dee holds up a finger and zaps a notebook and pen onto the coffee table. Cornelius jumps from the couch onto the table, picks up the pen with his tail, and starts writing.

"Wow," Bella says, peering around the cat. "Your lessons with him are really starting to pay off."

"That's because he's the smartest boy in the whole world, *yes he is,*" Dee coos. It's normal for witches to find creative ways to communicate with their familiars, but not many can successfully teach them to write. Such a task requires great patience and trust by both parties.

Bella, still watching Cornelius, cocks her head. "Is that supposed to say 'Eugene'?"

Dee sits up and takes the note, which looks like it was written by a small child. "He's still getting the hang of it," she reminds Bella, and then reads the note out loud. "It says, 'Youjeen grounded. No movy.'"

Dee squints at the paper. "I think that means Eugene is grounded and can't go to the movies tomorrow."

Cornelius meows happily at his job well done.

Bella scratches him on the head and then pulls her pink eyephone out of her pajama pocket. When the eye at the top of the screen opens, she says, "Call Eugene. Speakerphone."

Eugene picks up on the third ring. "Yes, I'm grounded," he says instead of hello. "For a week. The TrashEater6000 sort of backfired.

Two weeks' worth of trash exploded all over the kitchen." He lets out a heavy sigh. "Who'd have thought a machine could get indigestion?"

"So you can't come with us to the movies?" Dee whines. "But I need moral support!"

"Sorry, Dee. Nobody's more bummed than me. I love *Space Wars*." Eugene is obsessed with anything involving flying and laser beams.

"What about the flyball game on Friday?" Bella says. "It's my first game as scream team captain, and we're debuting some routines that will *really* get the crowd roaring."

"I'll try my best to be there. Maybe Mom will lighten my sentence for good behavior," Eugene says. "Speaking of which, I've gotta get back to cleaning up. Part of my punishment is that I have to get rid of the trash myself, instead of asking one of you to spell it away for me. Mom's got one of her eyes on the table, watching me."

Bella wrinkles her nose, grateful that neither of their dads are zombies.

"Okay," she says. "See you tomorrow at school." She hangs up.

"What a bummer." Dee slouches into the couch again as *Which Witch Is the One?* returns from commercial break. "At least you and Charlie will still be there." She scoops a handful of popcorn from the bowl on Bella's lap. "Maybe you'll even hit it off with one of Sebastian's friends."

"His human friends?" Bella scoffs. "Not likely."

"Come on, Bella," Dee urges. "Remember what Dad said? Don't judge a creature before you get to know them. Maybe they'll surprise you."

"I'm never surprised," Bella says. "Especially not by humans."

On the TV, Helena is crying in the back seat of a carriage. *"I've never let down my walls like this before, and it was all for nothing. Will I ever love again?"*

"Maybe you just need to let down your walls," Dee teases. Both sisters laugh, though deep down, Dee thinks there might be some truth to the idea. She wouldn't admit that to Bella, though. When it comes to matters of the heart, Bella can be more tightly wound than a mummy.

"Girls," they hear Ron calling out from his room upstairs. "You know what time it is."

"Boo," Bella calls out, and then points a finger at the TV and zaps it off. They don't need to bother trying to be sneaky by lowering the volume. As a werewolf, Ron has excellent hearing.

From his place on the coffee table, Cornelius meows and pushes the notebook forward with his paw. Dee picks it up and sees that he's written something else.

Giv catnip plees.

READ&
LEARN
with
simon kids

Looking for another great book?
Find it
IN THE MIDDLE.

Fun, fantastic books for kids
in the in-be**TWEEN** age.

IntheMiddleBooks.com